The
RELUCTANT
HUSBAND

ELIOT GRAYSON

Copyright © 2019 Eliot Grayson
All rights reserved.

No parts of this publication may be reproduced, stored in a retrieval system, or transmitted in any form or by any means, electronic, mechanical, photocopying, recording, or otherwise, without the prior written permission of the copyright owner.

This book is sold subject to the condition that it shall not, by way of trade or otherwise, be lent, resold, hired out, or otherwise circulated without the publisher's prior consent in any form of binding or cover other than that in which it is published and without a similar condition including this condition being imposed on the subsequent purchaser. Under no circumstances may any part of this book be photocopied for resale.

Cover design by Fiona Jayde

SMOKING
TEACUP
BOOKS

Published by Smoking Teacup Books
Los Angeles, California

ISBN: 9781076911131

Dedication

For Pete

I wish I could see your face right now.

Chapter One

"WELL, WELL," drawled a voice Tom knew and detested, a voice that raised all the fine hairs on the back of his neck. Why here, goddess, why now? Tom had come to this loud, smoky gaming hell in the least fashionable part of town specifically to avoid anyone he might know. "Tom Drake, as I live and breathe. Thought you were rusticating."

Face frozen in a rictus of a smile, Tom turned away from the faro table to face the owner of the voice, slapping his hand down over the two pitiful guineas left of the forty-three he'd had to his name when he stepped through the hell's doors. One of the coins went flying, pinging onto the floor and immediately disappearing in the chaos of the gaming room. His chest clenched, and he barely stopped himself from diving after it.

An ill-natured chuckle drew his attention back up. "Had a bad night, Drake?" The florid, grinning face of Marcus Leighton came into focus, far too close. The Leighton family tree had more twisted branches than a hawthorn. Must it really have been this member of their gods-forsaken family to pop up where he was least wanted? "Lost more than you could afford to?"

Everything he had, in fact, and more than just money. A hysterical laugh bubbled up, and he forced it down,

1

letting out a cough instead.

"Not at all," he said, his voice ringing distantly in his ears. "Just a trifle."

Leighton snickered, glancing down pointedly at the death grip Tom had on his one remaining guinea. "So I suppose you wouldn't mind buying an old school friend a brandy, eh?"

The man standing behind Leighton, until then in conversation with someone else, turned around to face them at that. "I wouldn't drink the brandy here, Marcus. Or should I say, the dyed gin?"

And that was simply the outside of enough, the final blow to bring Tom to his metaphorical knees. His real knees, too, had he not been still sitting on the faro-table's stool. Marcus Leighton had tormented him throughout his school days, mocking him for his enjoyment of books, his blue eyes, the way he shivered in the cold, and anything else he could think of, logical or not. His presence here, well — that was almost to be expected, given Tom's run of ill-luck. But his cousin Malcolm, the man beside him, had never taken the trouble. Far worse, he had never seemed to notice Tom at all. That Malcolm Leighton of all men should be witness to his final, degrading mortification was beyond anything Tom could have imagined.

Malcolm's cool, faintly amused expression didn't alter a whit as he looked Tom up and down, examining him as one might a not terribly interesting insect. "Drake, isn't it? Arthur Drake's brother?"

Tom flinched, cut to the quick. It didn't matter that he couldn't possibly know. At that moment, Tom was certain that he did, that his blasted cousin did, that every man in the room was laughing at his ruin and whispering over his estrangement from his family.

He rose abruptly, knocking into Marcus and making the man stumble and shout; he shoved past Malcolm and blindly forced his way through the crowd, leaving curses in his wake. Too many bodies, and faces, and the nauseating *smell* — harsh spirits and the reek of cigars, unwashed flesh and beneath it all, the rank scent of despair rising from too many men watching their fortunes and futures disappear.

Tom reached the door at last and burst into the comparatively quiet hallway, only a few men speaking discreetly here and there, either arranging assignations or discussing their debts. He bypassed the cloakroom and rushed past the mountain of a man guarding the front door, out onto the street.

"Sir? Are you taken ill?" the servant called out after him. Tom didn't stop. He stumbled down the side of the dingy square, tendrils of foul mist wreathing about his burning face, until he found an alcove in the side of a building where he could slump unseen and drop his head into his hands.

As he did, the last guinea slipped from his sweaty palm and tinkled away into the fog. Tom groaned and rubbed his forehead. He'd be damned if he was going to scrabble around on the filthy cobbles, where he'd likely never find it anyway. He might starve for it, but no. Let some street-sweeping urchin enjoy the windfall of a lifetime and feed his whole family on it for months. At least then Tom would have done something of benefit to someone else, even if accidentally.

Footsteps on the cobblestones of the square roused him from his fugue, and he pressed himself back into the alcove in panic. A lamp across the square did little to illuminate his corner; he was safe enough from anyone passing by.

Except that it wasn't just anyone, and he wasn't just passing by.

Malcolm Leighton stopped in the opening to the square, seeming to sense Tom's presence; his silhouette, sinister in the mist, sent a shiver down Tom's spine. But it was unmistakably Leighton, at least to one who'd spent years studying him surreptitiously from across school assemblies. He had a certain way of holding himself, both arrogant and graceful, that had always caught and held Tom's attention — had made it so bloody difficult for Tom to hide the feelings he had to keep out of sight at all costs. What his father might have done had he discovered Tom's leanings toward other men hadn't borne thinking of.

When Leighton turned, his face was in shadow, but Tom could easily imagine his expression: one corner of his mouth raised in cynical amusement, the slight lift of his thick, straight black brows, and the shrewd gleam of his dark eyes.

As he stepped closer Tom's body tightened, every muscle and tendon quivering with the urge to run, to fight, to take some *action*. He was cornered and brought to bay, quite literally and in every other way. If Leighton had followed him with violence in mind, he would find that Tom was not quite the easy pickings he had been as a schoolboy. Leighton still had an inch or two of height and the same in the breadth of his shoulders on Tom, but Tom could hold his own.

But when Leighton reached out, he held something in his hands, and his movements were slow and easy. "Your coat, Drake. They said you didn't have a hat."

The tension bled out of him as quickly as it had built, leaving him almost shaking from relief, from an odd disappointment, from despair and drink.

"You followed me to return my coat?" Tom's voice came out all wrong, hoarse and dry. He reached out, took the coat, felt its weight in his hands as something unfamiliar and strange, now that it had been in Leighton's possession even for a few minutes. "And — how did you know I'd left without it?"

"Half of the city saw you fly out the door as if all of Ingard's hounds were on your heels," Leighton drawled. "The gossips will be whispering of Tom Drake's sudden fit of madness, this time tomorrow."

"As though it matters," Tom muttered. He wished it didn't — wished he could be truly indifferent. He unfolded his coat, hands numb and clumsy, and nearly dropped it.

"Allow me." Leighton swept the coat away so smoothly that Tom hardly realized it was gone. "Well?" Leighton prompted him impatiently.

Tom left off gaping at him and turned obediently to allow Leighton to help him on with it, a task he accomplished as well as any valet Tom had ever had.

None of Tom's valets had ever lingered so long on the task of smoothing the fabric down his arms, though, nor stroked their hands over his hips afterward. Tom jerked away and spun to face Leighton.

"What the hell are you playing at?" he snarled. "If you

think I'm the kind of man to fumble in an alley —"

"I know you're that kind of man." Leighton pushed forward, his chest brushing Tom's and his face close enough that Tom could feel his breath. It was warm, and sweet with fine brandy, and nearly as intoxicating as the spirits Leighton had clearly imbibed. "But I'm not one to fumble, myself. There's a place nearby. Rooms to let, short notice and short term. I had thought to take you there."

"You're not *taking* me anywhere." Leighton's other meaning belatedly sank in. "And I don't fumble, in alleys or elsewhere, you arrogant, condescending, conceited arse!"

Leighton's broad shoulders moved slightly, an arrogant, condescending shrug if ever there was one. "Your rather checkered history says otherwise, Drake." Amused, Leighton was *amused* by Tom's misery, and it was suddenly the outside of enough.

Tom seized Leighton by the shoulders and shoved, knocking the bastard against the rough bricks of the alcove wall, and he followed the shove with his full weight, knocking Leighton back and pinning him. Leighton hit hard and let out an *oof* of surprise, his hat flying off and landing somewhere on the damp cobblestones of the walkway.

"Don't." Tom shook him once, slamming him into the wall. "Don't you dare speak of my wife as . . . checkered history. I should thrash you for that!"

"I'd like to see you try," Leighton retorted, as calmly as if they stood in a drawing room discussing the weather.

Tom had been thrashed more often than the reverse, most recently by his own brother, but he'd learned a thing or two on those occasions, most notably that one took what advantage one could and be damned to the rules. He drew back and drove his fist into Leighton's solar plexus — or would have, if Leighton hadn't caught his arm, ducked to the side like a damned snake, and used Tom's own momentum to fling him face-first into the wall.

He landed just hard enough to bruise, his cheek stinging where it scraped against the bricks. Leighton's full weight landed against his back and knocked the wind out of him. He only registered that Leighton had one arm twisted behind his back when he tried, and failed, to throw him off.

"That's enough of that," Leighton said, suddenly not sounding so amused. "A friendly quarrel is one thing. I draw the line at fisticuffs."

"We're not friends," Tom spat. He bucked, cursed, and landed against the wall again, winded and defeated.

Leighton leaned in, slowly pressing the whole length of his tall body against Tom's. "Certainly not," he breathed in Tom's ear, the warmth of it sending a contradictory shiver down his spine. "But the way you're wriggling your arse feels very friendly indeed."

Tom stilled abruptly; he had been moving, but surely that was just a continued attempt to loosen Leighton's hold.

"I didn't intend for you to stop," Leighton said, his low, smooth voice curling around the edges of Tom's confusion, soothing and lulling him, making everything hazy. "You have a delightful arse. It may be the only thing you have to recommend you."

Tom's eyes snapped open. The dull ochre of the wall

filled his vision; his own rasping breaths filled his ears; all his other senses could feel nothing but Leighton, on and around him, his rich, brandied scent and the heat of his hard form.

A harsh, horrible laugh rose up in his throat, and he forced it down before it could become a sob. His arse, of all things. His one remaining possession, besides a few items of clothing he couldn't appear before the world without and that he hadn't thought to sell — and that was all the value Leighton could see in him.

Goddess knew, perhaps that was all the value he had.

He squeezed his eyes shut, trying to fight the spinning of his head and the tingling in his extremities. He had to survive, didn't he? Everything he'd done had been what he'd had to do — he'd had no choice but to make the decisions he had. They'd all come out badly. His decisions always did, and this one would surely be no different.

But tomorrow he'd be hungry; within a week, he'd be evicted from his rooms. He needed to live. And the hat he'd pawned that morning had been one of Monsieur Favreau's masterpieces; gentlemen of higher station than Tom waited months for one made by the fellow's own hands. Really, he probably should have sold his arse first.

A strange calm descended as he made up his mind. "Let me go." And then, because Leighton seemed the sort to want to be quite sure he'd won, he added, "Please."

Leighton's hand around his wrist tightened, just a trifle, and then he released it and stepped away.

Tom took his time; he pushed back from the wall slowly enough to hide the stiffness in his limbs, and he carefully flicked the dust of the bricks from the front of his clothing. His fingers brushed over a snag in the silk of his last remaining waistcoat, and he shoved down the flash of panic at that. Leighton could afford to buy him another. He took a final moment before he turned around, giving himself one deep breath before he put his mask in place.

Bankrupt, disowned, and disheveled he might be, but Tom Drake could seduce anyone.

Chapter Two

"How much is it worth to you?" Mal blinked, but the vision before him didn't disappear. Drake had always been beautiful. Eyes blue as cornflowers, a smile that could melt the heart of a statue, and the way he moved that lean body — like a cat that tempted you to stroke it before sinking in its claws.

In this moment, he wasn't beautiful. He was wicked. Drake leaned back against the wall, one foot propped behind him, hands casually braced in his pockets and his hips tilted subtly forward in a way that would have had the whores who flocked the back rooms of the gaming hell they'd just left scurrying to take notes.

Mal stood perfectly straight and unmoving, hoping his tongue was still inside his mouth and his cockstand not too apparent. "I beg your pardon?"

Drake raised one perfectly arched brow. "My arse, Leighton," he all but purred. "How much is it worth to you?"

Mal's first impulse, to take mental stock of every penny he possessed, whether on his person or invested at the bank, couldn't possibly be right. No, horror and disgust would certainly be more appropriate than the teeth-clenching wave of desperate lust that swept over him as he imagined bending Drake over, taking what he wanted. The way Drake's slim hips would feel in his hands, the lines of smooth muscle in his back as he arched and moaned — no. No, and a thousand times no. He was not the sort of man —

"I'm certain we could come to some agreement," he said, voice embarrassingly hoarse.

It seemed he was indeed that sort of man, and Drake's slowly widening smile suggested he, at least, had known it all along.

Drake pushed off the wall and straightened his coat. "Lead the way, then."

Gods and goddesses, but this was a terrible idea. Mal covered his mounting nerves by executing a perfectly formal bow, waving Drake toward the square in a gesture as mocking as it was courtly. Drake's smile soured, but he sauntered out of the alley all the same, head held high.

Mal had to admire his poise. It was affected; it had to be, but it was all the more impressive for it. He fell into step beside Drake, the occasional brush of their arms enough to send sparks down his spine. He couldn't understand it. He'd had men, women, and a few intriguing individuals who were somewhere in between. None of them had captured and held his desire quite the way Drake did when Mal turned and saw him there, holding down his seat at the faro table like the last soldier in a siege.

Not that Drake didn't have a reputation for seduction. If the gossips could be believed, he'd left a swath of conquests in his wake, including an abandoned fiancé — now his own brother's husband, of all things — and a pregnant wife who had recently petitioned for a divorce, not an easy decision for a lady to make. None of the gods and goddesses whose temples officiated marriages made much trouble over granting divorces, but society could be savage in its condemnation of those who pursued one. Both fiancé and wife had clearly succumbed to Drake's charms and quickly learned to regret it.

Mal suspected he would fare no better. It didn't matter. He would have tonight, and face his regrets in the morning. They could join all his others in a chorus of recrimination.

They crossed the square in silence, a few other small groups of men passing wraith-like in the soupy fog. Distant laughter echoed oddly off bricks and cobblestones, and the streetlamps at the edges of the square gave it all a dim, unearthly glow. Mal felt that he'd slipped into another world, that perhaps Drake wasn't human, but some faerie being who had appeared tonight to drag him out of his normal plane of existence. Would he even be paying Drake in simple gold, or in something less tangible he could ill afford to lose?

Lost in his thoughts, Mal nearly missed their turn, and he had to grasp Drake by the arm to bring him up short.

"It's just down this way," he said, and turned them toward a narrow street that led away from the main thoroughfare. Drake's muscles bunched beneath his fingers, reassuringly masculine and real. He didn't let go, and Drake didn't pull away.

Mal peered into the gloom, looking closely at doorways until he stopped before the blue-painted door he knew well enough from previous assignations.

He lifted the iron knocker and thumped it once against the door; a panel slid aside, and after a moment's scrutiny by a pair of sharp dark eyes, the hinges creaked and the door swung open. The hallway beyond was hardly prepossessing. Narrow and lit only by a pair of candles in tarnished brass sconces, it led to a plain, uncarpeted staircase. Drake's arm tensed beneath Mal's hand, and he tightened his grip. No bloody chance that he'd let Drake scarper now.

Mal nodded at the doorman, who'd been here on the several other occasions he'd made use of the house's services. Half a crown changed hands, and the man produced a candle and a heavy key tagged with a number from a small cupboard set into the wall to the right of the door. Mal pocketed the key while the man lit the candle, and then he and Drake were mounting the stairs.

Slowly, because Drake seemed determined to drag his feet. "Leighton," he whispered, sounding very young and far less sure of himself than he had when offering himself a few minutes before. "Are you certain —"

"Yes." Mal ignored the twinge of guilt that would have had him stop. "Don't be a milksop. There are rooms to let upstairs, not a torture chamber, or whatever nonsense you're imagining."

A quick, indrawn breath was his only answer.

At the top of the stairs, two passages stretched out in opposite directions. It was rather better lit up here, and less bare, with paper on the walls and a strip of drugget running the length of the corridor. Mal led them to the fourth room on the left, and then he hesitated, candle in one hand and Drake in the other.

Drake wordlessly held out his free hand for the candle so that Mal wouldn't need to let go of him, and Mal flushed, biting his lip. Was he so very transparent? Instead of handing it over, he dropped Drake's arm, almost roughly, and pulled the key from his pocket. Drake's low, mocking laugh eradicated anything left of his better feelings. Drake was a callous seducer himself, and turnabout was fair play.

The bedroom was just as Mal had expected: plain but clean, with a small coal fire in the grate and a bottle of gin set with two glasses on the cheap deal sideboard. Mal locked the door behind them and set the candle beside the gin, turning to find Drake already shedding his coat and draping it over the room's one chair.

He stared for a moment, lost in the sight of Drake bending to remove his boots and stockings. He was turned to the side, depriving Mal of the sight of his backside, but the play of muscle in his shoulders and flanks mesmerized him all on its own.

Drake glanced up and fixed Mal with his bright, too-blue eyes. "Well?" he drawled. "Do you mean to remain clothed for the duration?"

Mal forced himself to shake off his odd mood — a mix of unwilling lust, and shame, and the feeling of having passed into some strange dream where he had no influence over events.

"Eager, are you?" he replied, with a sneer.

Drake flushed, but the glitter of his eyes spelled trouble. That wasn't humiliation, that was anger, and Mal delighted in it. Drake was as much a man of the world as he, and no victim, now or ever. Mal need not hesitate.

And he didn't. He crossed the few feet separating them and caught Drake by the chin, fingers digging into his jaw and angling it just so — tipped up just enough that Drake knew who was in control.

"Not to worry," he said, his voice gone low and rough. "I'm eager enough myself." And he leaned in and caught Drake's mouth with his own.

It was sweeter than he'd allowed himself to imagine, and soft, but Drake's kiss was anything but. He used his mouth with skillful intent, giving back as much as he took, his tongue darting out to explore Mal's mouth. He was clearly a man used to taking charge of a kiss, and that wouldn't do. That wouldn't do at all. Mal wanted nothing more than to make Drake give in. He wanted him yielding, desperate, lost in Mal's touch, unable to do more than take what Mal gave him.

He wrapped his free arm around Drake's back and yanked their bodies flush, thrusting one thigh between Drake's legs and pulling him off balance. Drake caught at his shoulders to steady himself, and *there*, that was better, that was just as it ought to be — until Drake used those hands on his shoulders to shove him. Mal stumbled back a step, his lower lip stinging from where Drake had *bitten* him, the bastard.

"What the fuck do you think you're doing?" he growled. "Are you mad?"

Drake stared him down, his chest heaving, his eyes gleaming almost feverishly in the flickering candlelight. "I'm not a woman," he said, voice raw. "I'm not some dainty little plaything for you to — manhandle as you please!"

There was something there, something more than just indignation at a little rough handling, but irritation overwhelmed Mal's curiosity.

"I know damn well you're not a woman," he snapped. "I had your prick pressed against my leg a moment ago. And," he went on when Drake looked like he might say more, "I wouldn't be so coarse as to manhandle someone dainty or little. Nor does being manhandled make you less of a man, even when the one doing the — manhandling is a man —" Mal stuttered into silence, abruptly aware of how utterly ridiculous he sounded.

Drake's outrage had faded into a smirk; clearly he agreed. Mal flushed with mortification, but perhaps it was just as well. The furious, defensive tension in Drake's posture had eased.

Mal prowled closer again. "Bending over says nothing about your worth," he said, carefully avoiding any word that contained the syllable *man*. "Or if it does, it only says that you're worth fucking."

"Charming," Drake muttered, but when Mal pulled him into his arms again, he didn't resist. The moment his lips touched Drake's again, Mal forgot all of it: his awkwardness, Drake's anger, everything but the heat between them, the hard muscles of Drake's chest pressed against his own, the nearly overwhelming urge to fling Drake against the wall and simply take him.

Instead he turned them, gripping Drake hard by the hips and then shoving him onto the bed. Mal landed on top without breaking the kiss, his hands roaming everywhere, mapping the angles and curves of Drake's lean, supple body.

Drake shoved at his coat, and Mal had to pull back long enough to let it slide unheeded to the floor. He stopped for a moment, transfixed, staring down at Drake's red, swollen lips, the flush on his cheeks, the disheveled mess of his hair, a few strands gleaming gold amidst the dark mass. Difficult to remember that Drake wasn't the sort of man one could trust, or love, or even like; Mal *wanted*, with such an ache he could hardly bear it.

He reached out and stroked his fingers gently down the side of Drake's face, feeling the softness of his skin, the faint rasp of stubble. Drake turned his head and bit his fingertips, hard.

Mal jerked his hand back. "You —"

"Get on with it," Drake snapped, his tone a little belied by his breathlessness. "We're not here to gaze at one another, are we?"

The tenderness that had welled up in him withered instantly. "Fine. Get your damn clothes off, then." He grasped Drake's breeches and tugged them down, several of the buttons ripping through their buttonholes and one of them flying off and clicking to the floorboards.

"You're a bastard, that was my last good set of breeches," Drake gasped, but he sat up enough to pull his shirt over his head in one swift motion. Mal threw the breeches after the button and gave Drake's drawers the same treatment.

And then Drake lay before him, every inch of him on display. Broad shoulders tapered to a narrow waist, slim hips meant for Mal's hands to grip, a lovely long cock that had Mal's mouth watering, and long, endlessly long legs, that Mal could so easily imagine wrapped around him.

Mal needed to undress himself, but that could wait — and the thought of fucking Drake while fully dressed, just his cock out, with Drake nude beneath him, made him nearly come in his breeches. He needed a taste, first, before anything. Mal put his hands on Drake's smooth, creamy thighs and pushed them open, drawing a sound of protest; he leaned down — and he froze as if he'd been turned to stone.

It wasn't easy to see by the light of a single candle, but it was nonetheless unmistakable. There, at the very top of Drake's right thigh, almost in the crease where his leg met his groin, was a slate-gray mark: the sigil of the goddess Mirreith, imprinted on Tom's skin and indelibly marking him as one of her chosen.

Mal's mind whirled, all his desires suddenly unimportant, all his plans reforming in an instant.

"Well," he said. "It seems you have something besides your arse to recommend you after all."

Chapter Three

Tom's heart beat so hard and fast against his ribs that his vision blurred. He tried to jerk his legs from Leighton's grasp, but the bastard held firm, spreading him open and staring intently down at that thrice-damned mark, his dark eyes gone black.

He had meant to keep his drawers on, to turn over and pull them down over his hips just enough to expose the only part of him Leighton would care about. He'd planned it out on the walk to this miserable place, how he'd distract Leighton with his hands and mouth, drive him to distraction until he'd have no attention to spare for anything Tom didn't want him to see.

And that plan had vanished like so much smoke from the goddess's temple censers the moment Leighton put his hands on him. At his father's insistence, not even his brother Arthur knew about the goddess's mark on him. Years, a lifetime of hiding his shame — all gone in a moment, because Tom didn't have the strength to resist Leighton's knowing touch and the effortless dominance of his kisses.

"Let go," he said, finding his voice at last. "Let me go."

Leighton tore his eyes away from the mark, his gaze pinning Tom like prey. Slowly, he moved his hands away, and he sat back on the bed, still watching Tom like a hawk would a mouse. Tom scrabbled back, pulling the bedclothes over his lap and feeling far more exposed than even his nudity would warrant. He shivered, not from cold but from the pure shock of it. Leighton knew. *Everyone* would know, because this would be one of the best on-dits of the year. How could Leighton resist spreading it far and wide? And why would he want to? Tom was nothing to him; less than nothing, someone he held in utter contempt.

"You married a woman," Leighton said, bewildered. "You were engaged before that, were you not? To another man with Mirreith's blessing. You truly are mad."

Tom wanted to argue, to deny, to throw out some snarling retort that would make Leighton take his coat and go. But he could think of nothing to say to that simple statement of fact. Tom had never paid too much attention as a child to the rambling of the priestesses about legends and mystical nonsense; he had passionately wished, with all his boyish heart, that it had nothing whatever to do with him.

But he knew Mirreith's history in its outline. Mirreith ruled the sea, and her rivals were Ingard and Engar, twin goddess and god of the shore, the cliffs and rocks and beaches. They quarreled, and Mirreith threw herself against the land, raging with all the furious might of the waves. It was a sporting effort, Tom had always thought, but in the end the land remained and the twins triumphed. The priestesses always glossed over the way Mirreith paid forfeit for her defeat, with high-sounding euphemisms about *giving of herself* and *subjugating her strength to the will of the divine*.

Reading between the lines, Tom suspected Mirreith

had lain down on the beach and been quite spectacularly and divinely fucked by both Engar and Ingard, whether at once or in tandem. In any case, ever since then Mirreith's chosen had been blessed, yes, but they remained under Mirreith's protection only so long as they did as she had been forced to, and yielded to another in body and soul. Ingard demanded it as a permanent reminder to Mirreith's worshippers of her defeat.

It appeared that Leighton had attended to his theological instruction in his youth, damn him. He knew as well as Tom did that one who carried Mirreith's blessing did not enter into the sorts of marriages Tom had tried twice to do. If men or women with her blessing tried to marry one another, or anyone of either sex who couldn't *subjugate their strength* properly, their luck turned to a curse.

"Well?" Leighton prompted him. "*Are* you mad, or merely stupid?"

"It's no business of yours," Tom said. "It doesn't matter. You should go." He hated the defeat in his own voice; he hated how sulky he sounded even more. But he was quite done. He had thought to take a measure of control over his fate, tonight, to extract enough funds from Leighton to go — somewhere. Somewhere else. Somewhere no one knew him, and he could start afresh.

It was doomed, of course. He could never leave what he was behind, no matter how he struggled and raged and pleaded with a goddess who had abandoned him for his transgressions. And now Leighton knew, and he had nothing, not even his secret.

Leighton sat back and settled at the end of the bed, one

knee bent and the other leg dangling over. He looked quite at his ease. His speculative expression, with narrowed eyes and pursed lips, left Tom decidedly less so. He couldn't rise and dress without standing nude before Leighton's all-too-knowing scrutiny, which left him trapped, the bedcovers drawn up about his chest.

"And what if it were my business?" Leighton asked at last. "What if I wanted to make it so?"

A laugh rose up, leaving Tom's throat raw from the bitterness of it. "If you're thinking of blackmailing me, you're a deal too late. I have nothing to give. Or have you already forgotten you meant to pay me for a fuck tonight?"

Leighton cocked his head thoughtfully. "You have your reputation. Or I should say, what tattered remnants you've managed to keep about you."

"I've no use for a reputation when I'm going to be starving by tomorrow." Tom snapped his mouth shut, horrified at what had slipped out of his mouth.

"Those may be the first true words you've spoken to me tonight." Leighton leaned forward, fixing Tom with his dark gaze, looking more serious than Tom had ever seen him. "You're not going to starve if I help you. And I will help you, if you're honest with me now. Are you divorced?"

Tom stared at him a moment, utterly flummoxed. "Why on earth would you care one way or the other?"

"Humor me," Leighton said firmly. "I mean it. Answer my questions, and I'll help you. My word as a gentleman."

He hesitated, but really, was there any reason to lie? Or refuse to answer, even? Leighton had uncovered the one thing Tom had truly kept from the world, and as for the rest, the gossips would know it all soon enough. "Caroline petitioned Ingard's temple, where we were married. The priestesses are granting it, but they're waiting until she —" Tom swallowed, his throat thick, "until she bears our child."

Leighton frowned, and his whole body appeared to tense. "And that will be…?"

"Within the fortnight, if the midwife who examined her early on was correct about the date of conception."

The set of Leighton's shoulders relaxed. "Soon, then. You could marry again as soon as a few weeks from now."

"Marry again? Why in the names of all the gods would I want to? And it's not as if I have a line of suitors and languishing young ladies waiting for me to —" He broke off abruptly. Surely not. "You don't mean you. You can't possibly."

A mocking grin lit up Leighton's saturnine face, transforming it into something impossibly attractive, just for a moment. "Very good, Drake. I thought your brother had all the brains in the family, but you're not such a slow top after all."

Tom had proposed marriage twice in his life, once in frantic, reckless desperation to escape the grasp of fate, and once because his would-be father-in-law would have beaten him bloody and dropped him in the river if he hadn't. Even so, he'd managed to be relatively polite and even complimentary on both occasions. This was beyond the pale.

"Go fuck yourself, Leighton. And Arthur with you. I wouldn't marry you even if you kept me in silk and champagne for eternity."

"Superfine and brandy, then, if you'd rather live like a gentleman than a trollop," Leighton snapped, flushing brick red. "Get off your high horse. You've gone against every stricture of your patron goddess. You're pockets to let, your wife's divorcing you, your family's cast you out from what I hear — and don't think I won't have all the details of that out of you in good time — and your other option is to starve in a gutter somewhere. Or sell that lovely body of yours to someone a deal less courteous than I am."

For just a moment, Tom's mind snagged on entirely the wrong part of that. Leighton thought he was lovely? No, no, and damn it, no. He didn't care what Leighton thought, and what in blazes was the *matter* with him?

"You consider yourself courteous? You're delusional. And I will not marry you." If his voice wavered a little, along with his resolution, he hoped it was subtle enough to escape Leighton's notice.

Leighton opened his mouth, shut it, and then sighed. "Forgive me."

Tom could hardly credit his senses. "I think you'll need to be more specific," he said, before Leighton could continue.

That earned him a glare. "For proposing marriage in such a clumsy manner," he grated out. "Not for anything else. I quite categorically do *not* ask your forgiveness for anything else."

Tom drew the sheets a little more tightly around his waist and returned the glare as well as he could, considering. "If you want me to forgive you, you'll need to do rather better the next time." Leighton raised one thick black brow, and Tom hurried on before he could comment on the way Tom had just contradicted himself. If he wouldn't marry Leighton under any circumstances, suggesting he ask again was rather absurd. "Anyway, you're not the only one with questions. Why do you want to marry me at all? You could have what you want for a few guineas and a supper."

"Because fucking you isn't what I want." Tom raised his own eyebrows at that. "Yes, yes," Leighton said, waving a hand in dismissal. "I do want to fuck you. And I will fuck you, have no doubt about that." Leighton stopped, biting his lip, and Tom knew he had him. Leighton had a secret of his own, something that meant he needed Tom every bit as much as Tom needed what Leighton had to give. He waited with bated breath.

Finally, Leighton went on in a rush, "But I need a god's blessing, I need it quickly, and you're in need of everything. Marry me, and we'll both get what we lack."

Tom took a moment to consider, and then another moment to appear to be considering — and then, as Leighton began to look as if he might explode, yet another, just to show he could.

"You need Mirreith's blessing," he said slowly. "Or some blessing, at any rate. And I can't imagine you haven't searched. You've looked for a wife or a husband who bears a god's mark, and you haven't found one, have you?"

Leighton's strained, angry silence was answer enough. Thirteen gods and goddesses were commonly worshipped in the Isles, and all of them gave blessings — but sparingly. There might be fewer than ten infants born with each god's blessing a year. They were often in high demand as spouses once of an age, since their families by birth or marriage were under their patron deities' protection.

"And here I am," Tom went on, "offered up to you on a platter. But I could say no. And the look on your face tells me you might need me more than I need you. I can find another man to pay for my favors —"

"The hell you will!" Leighton exclaimed with surprising force, and then stopped, looking as shocked as Tom felt.

"Why, Leighton," Tom said, with saccharine sweetness and an exaggerated flutter of his lashes. "I didn't know you cared."

Leighton scowled, but he couldn't quite meet Tom's eyes. "I don't. But you should marry me instead. You know it's the better choice, for any reason you can think of." He looked up then, and there was something troubled, something dark in his eyes that drained away all of Tom's annoyance and mockery. "Name your terms, Drake. I'll meet them. Any settlement you like. I can afford it. We can live wherever you wish, we can fill a lake with wine and hold orgies in the woods for all I care, only marry me as soon as you're free."

Tom couldn't help laughing at that. Leighton was clearly no prude, but he wasn't the sort to run naked in the forest, either, and the idea was too absurd.

"My cousin is dying, Drake." Leighton spoke so quietly Tom almost missed his words even in the room's silence. "Not bloody Marcus, I might be sorry for that but only in theory. William. My cousin Will. He was in the form below you at school, do you remember? He's my heir, and my closest friend, and he's dying."

Tom did remember William, a pleasant, friendly lad with ears too large for his head and a tendency to laugh at inappropriate moments. He remembered, too, how devoted he always was to his elder cousin, and Leighton's reciprocal kindness. None of the boys had ever picked on William Leighton — or rather, none more than once. Malcolm Leighton had been tall for his age, and vicious when he wanted to be.

"I'm sorry," he said, all traces of laughter vanished. "Truly, Leighton. He's a decent fellow, always was."

"And he still will be," Leighton said, eyes gleaming, "if I can bring a blessing into the family. He's my direct heir. The blessing would apply to him as well, not just to me."

"I'm not so certain it works like that —"

"It *must* work like that!" Leighton all but shouted. He stopped and ran his hand down over his face. Tom's heart gave an odd twist. Leighton had never been one to show his feelings, nor even his thoughts. At fourteen he had been as cynical and as composed as a jaded roué twice his age, and he'd only grown into it since. But now he looked wrecked, his desperation written in every feature. "Drake, it must work like that. Gods only know, I've tried everything else. Every city specialist, every strange foreign cure, I've given a dragon's hoard of gold to every temple in the country. He has months, at most, the most trustworthy of the doctors believe. I'd die in his place if I could. He's a better man than I could ever be."

Leighton's voice broke at that, and Tom's resolution broke with it. The Leighton cousins were, in many ways, more true and more affectionate brothers than Tom and

Arthur had ever been. Perhaps if Tom had ever found the courage to tell Arthur the truth about himself, they could have been more to each other; he regretted that now, more than ever, since Arthur had cut him out of his life for good. Even now, the thought of Arthur dying of some incurable sickness struck him with a bone-deep horror.

Tom's blessing would, according to Mirreith's temple's official pronouncements, extend to Leighton and to his cousin. Whether that blessing would be enough for a miracle was another question entirely. It was foolish to tie their lives together for such a tenuous hope. Foolish, and reckless, and likely to end in disaster.

"Yes," Tom said. "I'll marry you." Foolish, reckless, and likely to end in disaster — how could he say no?

Chapter Four

TOM FROWNED at his reflection, moving back and forth to see himself in sections in the small, chipped mirror. He didn't have time to tie his cravat properly, and his hair was mussed, and damn Leighton anyway for dropping by unexpectedly.

And damn himself for caring what Leighton thought. He wasn't Leighton's lover; since they'd agreed to marry, Leighton hadn't touched him, not even to the extent of a casual hand on his arm. That Leighton had given him funds sufficient to pay his landlord, eat like a king, and entirely renew his wardrobe was quite beside the point. One couldn't be a light-skirt — light-breeches? — if one didn't bed one's patron, could one? And if Leighton didn't want him, then Tom certainly didn't want Leighton. He had his pride, although that pride bent a bit in the middle of the night, when he tossed and turned alone in his narrow bed and took himself in hand to lull himself to sleep. Best not to think about that just before he faced the man, though.

He had just given his coat one final twitch, to make it lay just so around his waist, when a brisk knock sounded on the door of the little sitting room he rented along with an even smaller bedchamber.

Tom threw himself into the faded armchair by the

window, affecting a casual pose, though his heart pounded rather less casually. "Just come in, why don't you. You know you'll stroll in as if you own the place anyway —"

He broke off abruptly and leapt to his feet as the door opened to admit a man who was decidedly not Leighton. He had never seen the fellow in his life, and would certainly have remembered if he had. Wheat-blond hair, striking dark eyes, and a tall, trim figure wrapped in a very smartly tailored coat made him rather unforgettable. Tom hadn't even thought to ask the housemaid to elaborate when she'd told him a gentleman was there to see him, because who else would visit him? All of his bridges had not been just burned, but ground into powder and the ashes salted.

The stranger raised his eyebrows and tapped his hat against his leg, somehow questioning Tom's manners and sanity without saying a single word.

Tom drew himself up to his full height, which he thought might be almost the same as his visitor's, if he had taller shoes. It would have to do. "I'm afraid you have the advantage of me, sir. What is your name and business with me?"

"John Cook," the man said shortly, and then after a pause, as if he'd expected that to be enough, "A solicitor. With Honeyfield and Cook. I believe you are acquainted with the firm's senior partner." Of course he was; Mr. Honeyfield had almost become his father-in-law, before Owen Honeyfield had married Tom's brother in his place.

But Owen was not Tom's concern at the moment. All the blood rushed out of his head, and he had to catch himself on the back of his chair. "Are they — are they well?

All of them? My wife? Our — goddess, please tell me she and our child —" He couldn't continue, couldn't even ask what he so desperately longed to know. The thought of becoming a father had seemed so very abstract, even when he'd spent every day with Caroline as she increased, earlier in her pregnancy. Now it struck him with visceral force. He had conceived a child with his wife, and now he was dependent upon this stranger for news of whether they even lived.

Cook's lip curled in obvious disgust. "You ought to be on the stage, Drake. I wish I could walk out of here and leave you in suspense; no doubt you'd forget all about it within the hour. But it is my duty to tell you that Mrs. Drake gave birth to a son the night before last. Alexander Owen Drake and his mother are both well, as I am sure you will be deeply relieved," he gave those last two words a distinctly sarcastic twist, "to know."

Tom's head buzzed with relief, with joy, with grief, with utter humiliation. He ought to have been there. There was no room in his mind for any other thought, save *I ought to have been there*, drumming within him to the rhythm of his racing pulse.

He dropped back into the chair. "Thank the goddess. Thank —" Tom put his head in his hands, and breathed deeply until he thought he could look up without fainting. "Did Arthur send you?"

"No," Cook said briskly. "Caroline did."

Every muscle in Tom's body clenched. "Remember to whom you're speaking, you insolent upstart," he hissed. "I am Mrs. Drake's husband, and you'll speak of her with proper respect."

Cook stared at him for a moment, and then burst out laughing. "And you're the one to school me in showing *Mrs. Drake* the proper respect, are you? Don't play the fool. You *were* her husband in name only, and this," he said as he brandished a portfolio Tom hadn't noticed tucked under his arm, "is the divorce decree issued by the Temple of Ingard this morning."

"Oh, thank the goddess," burst out of Tom's mouth. Leighton had called the day before, haggard and drawn and bearing news of a sudden downturn in William's condition, and Tom's first thought was of him.

Cook reared back, wrinkling his nose as if at a foul odor. "Caroline will be delighted to hear how pleased you are to be well shot of her and her son."

"It's not that," Tom cried, aghast and furious in equal measure. Goddess, he had no wish to justify himself to this jumped-up tradesman, but he would carry the tale back to Caroline, back to Arthur. "This divorce was no choice of mine, but circumstances —"

"Yes, I can imagine the circumstances," Cook said scathingly. "No doubt you have some other dupe already on the string. Or more than one, given your past history."

"I'm sure Caroline and Owen would be so very flattered by your description of them," Tom snarled, cut to the quick — the more so because Cook was rather too close to the truth. "Perhaps I ought to let them know how little you think of them."

Cook turned a satisfying red at that, but he rallied quickly. "As if they would believe a word out of your mouth, Drake. And they are both well aware that you took advantage of their good natures. That is not to their discredit, but to yours."

Tom floundered for a reply for a critical moment; Cook clearly understood how perfect a parting shot that was. Without another word, he extracted the divorce decree from his portfolio, dropped it on the table, and left the room, shutting the door with a decided slam.

MAL WALKED to Drake's rooms, glad of the chance to clear his head. The near hour that it took, even with his long legs and quick stride, was still not nearly enough to achieve that aim. Will kept up a brave front, but he looked like a man thrice his age, his hair thin and lank, his eyes sunken, and his once-athletic body nearly skeletal. Mal had ridden out of the city to visit him that morning, and galloped back again as if Ingard's hunt were riding after him.

He and Drake had to marry, and soon. They were out of time; Will was out of time. The doctors tried to hem and haw, but it was a matter of weeks before Will succumbed to the disease eating him alive from the inside out.

Mal had waited as patiently as he could for Drake's divorce to be issued, but waiting was no longer an option. He would drag Drake by the ear to his brother's estate and force him to demand the divorce himself if he had to.

Drake's boardinghouse wasn't in a fashionable part of town, but it was safe enough that Mal didn't trouble to keep to the main thoroughfares. He took ten minutes off the journey by cutting through a warren of alleys. Brushing past the startled housemaid, he took the stairs to Drake's rooms two at a time. He could all but feel Will's life running out, like sand slipping through an hourglass, and marrying Drake would turn the hourglass. It had to.

Mal knocked quickly before simply letting himself in, and then he stopped, blinking at the darkness. Drake was home; the housemaid had assured him of that. But not a candle was lit, there were only a few embers in the fireplace, and Drake was nowhere to be seen. Mal felt his way to the fireplace and held the wick of a candle to the coals. The flame took, and Mal held it out, casting a wavering glimmer over the sitting room.

He had never entered Drake's bedroom, but it looked as if he would need to now. He crossed the room, a little unnerved by the silence. On each of his other visits, Drake had been waiting for him in the sitting room, a glass of brandy in hand and some drawling commentary on Mal's appearance or habits on his lips; he was almost never silent.

The bedroom door swung open at his touch, and Mal lifted the candle. The room had no other illumination. At first he thought the housemaid must have been mistaken. And then he saw Drake, a lump beneath the bedcovers, looking almost like a rumpled quilt himself.

"Drake?" Mal's voice echoed in the stillness. "Drake?" He crossed to the bed, concerned now, and shook what he thought might be Drake's shoulder. Concern became alarm as Drake showed no signs of life. Mal set the candle on the nightstand and knelt on the side of the bed, gripping Drake's torso and heaving him onto his back.

Slowly, Drake's eyes opened and fixed him with a glassy stare. "What do you want?" he said at last, the words oddly slurred, as though spoken through lips gone numb.

"What do you think I bloody well want?" Mal demanded, fury taking hold now that he knew Drake was alive and well enough. What was the bastard playing at? "I want to marry, as quickly as possible. The same thing I always want. Have you any news?"

Another slow blink, and then Drake closed his eyes and tried to roll to his side again. Mal hauled him back and shook him by the shoulders, making his head bounce against the pillows. "Damn you, open your eyes and say something! Are you ill, or only drunk?"

"Not drunk," Drake mumbled. Mal believed him; he couldn't smell spirits, and if drunkenness had accounted for Drake's condition, he would have reeked like a distillery.

"What, then? Do I need to summon a physician? Tell me what ails you before I lose my patience and douse you with a bucket of water." Mal wasn't quite certain he could induce the housemaid to give him one for the purpose, but he wasn't above making the attempt.

Drake looked up at him, and Mal was horrified to see the sheen of tears. Gods, no, not that. Tears were his weakness; tears in a pair of eyes as pretty as Drake's would have him on his knees within minutes, begging to kill someone on the man's behalf.

"Drake. For the gods' sakes, Tom," he said, hating his own weakness, but helpless before the single drop that tracked down Drake's pale cheek. "Will you only tell me what's the matter? If you're ill, I'll fetch whatever you need. You should have sent for me."

"I'm not ill," Drake murmured, still in the same strange, dreamy way. "Not ill. I'm glad you're here. The div—divorce decree is in there." A slight movement beneath the blankets might have been Drake's attempt at a wave.

Mal's anger came roaring back in full force. The decree was final, was there, and Drake had been lying in his bed in whatever state he was in, rather than letting him know at once? He knew there was not a moment to lose. He knew, and he clearly didn't give a damn. Drake let out a pitiful sound, and Mal realized his hands had tightened on Drake's shoulders to the point of bruising.

He let go and stood abruptly, with a sound of disgust. "In the sitting room? The decree."

"Yes," Drake said, after an infuriating pause.

Mal stormed into the next room, barked his shin on the chair, cursed, and stormed back to the bedroom. He collected the candle and stomped back again, angrier than ever. The decree was there, sitting on the table, easily overlooked as just another one of the letters and newspapers Drake tended to strew about on every surface. Mal snatched it up, putting it close enough to his face to make it out in the dim light of the candle.

He read it through once, and then again, and finally dropped into the armchair, feeling like a marionette left abandoned by its maker. The divorce was final; Drake was free to marry again, and had been as of that morning.

Mal's anger ratcheted up and up, until he felt his blood might boil out of his veins. They could have married that afternoon. Will could die any moment—and Drake had lounged in his bed, unconcerned, as precious hours slipped by.

Mirreith's priestesses preferred to perform ceremonies

during the day, but sufficient donations to the temple funds, Mal had found, worked wonders in overcoming such small matters of protocol. He took the candle over to Drake's small desk and rummaged through the detritus until he found a pencil and a scrap of paper; a note to his butler demanding a carriage and the immediate delivery of every penny in the household funds was written in a moment. A quick jaunt to the downstairs hall and a shilling in the housemaid's hand ensured it would be carried at once by the girl's suitor, a butcher's apprentice who was conveniently hanging about by the kitchen door.

That done, it was time to deal with Drake.

Chapter Five

MAL DIDN'T BOTHER with a bucket of water; instead, he simply charged into Drake's bedchamber and jerked the bedclothes from him, flinging them to the floor in a heap. When Drake didn't so much as stir, Mal finally and completely lost his temper.

It wasn't something that happened often; he prided himself on his control of his feelings. But this — this indifference, or apathy, or carelessness, or whatever it was that had Drake in its grip — this was the absolute outside of enough.

"Up!" he roared, loud enough to rouse everyone in the house. He grasped Drake by the arm and pulled him up, then wrapped an arm about his waist and tugged him bodily out of the bed. Drake let out a little moan. Mal ruthlessly stamped out his momentary, guilty flicker of compassion. "Stand up and dress, and bloody well snap out of it!"

At last, Drake seemed to become conscious of his surroundings; he pulled away and stumbled, catching himself against the nightstand with a rattle and thump. He stared at Mal, eyes wide, pupils so large that black nearly drowned out the blue of his irises.

"What," he rasped, swallowing hard. "What's the matter?"

"I have been asking you that this half hour," Mal gritted out. "What — the very devil — have you been doing, lying in bed when you know that Will may have only days to live? Why didn't you send for me at once?"

Drake rubbed shaking hands over his face. "I didn't think of it," he said, muffled behind them. "I'm sorry. I didn't think."

"I don't suppose you're capable of it," Mal spat. "You never think. And so I'm quite done offering you the opportunity to do so. Make yourself presentable, or don't for all I care, but in five minutes we're going to be married. And after that, we're going straight to see Will, and we're staying there until he's well again."

"Tonight?" Drake asked bewilderedly. "But the temples close at sundown —"

"And they open again when you're offering a small fortune for them to do so. Dress. Five minutes. If you're not ready, I'll throw you over my shoulder and carry you."

Drake made a weak attempt to glare at him. "I don't suppose you're capable of it."

Mal smiled sourly and advanced a few menacing steps. He took great satisfaction in the way Drake flinched and pressed himself back against the nightstand at his approach. "Don't try me."

He turned on his heel and left the room, slamming the door shut behind him. Let Drake use some of his precious five minutes finding and lighting a candle in the darkness of his bedchamber. Mal needed the one lit candle to show the way to Drake's bottle of brandy in the interim.

THE ONLY SOUND in the darkened room was Tom's own breathing, harsh and raspy and far too loud in the silence. His head swam sickeningly. When he closed his eyes, strange colored spots formed, and when he opened them, the dark had a throbbing quality that made his eyes hurt and his balance shift. He clutched the edge of the nightstand in fingers that felt too weak to support him. How long had he laid in his bed after Cook left that morning? He hardly remembered. It must have been eight or ten hours, but it might as well have been as many days; his limbs were heavy and limp, as they would have felt after a long run of fever.

The clink of glass against glass and a muffled curse told him that Leighton was still in the sitting room. Tom knew he was in no state to put up a fight if Leighton chose to drag him out, half dressed and unshod; he was equally unfit to dress and make ready, certainly not quickly. The task of finding a candle was overwhelming enough to make him want to collapse to the floor and curl up in a ball.

And he didn't care enough either way, that was the plain fact of it. He didn't care if he was married in his boots and coat, or without them; he didn't want to fight Leighton. It was a matter of complete indifference to him whether he married or not, or ate supper or not, or spent the rest of his life in his bed with the sheets drawn up over his face.

That indifference struck him like a profound revelation. He marveled at it for a moment, at the avenue of total freedom he'd opened up from the world and its cares, from Leighton, from Arthur and Caroline and Owen, from his newborn son — a faint pang there, he noted almost distantly — and from himself and his own innumerable failings.

He proposed to Owen knowing full well it would be disastrous. Two blessed individuals of either sex were begging for trouble if they tried to marry. But propose he did, in a panicked, desperate attempt to hide from his own fate. He lost Owen by bedding Caroline while away on a trip to the city, supposedly preparing for the wedding and in reality losing himself in any debauchery available. Marrying Caroline was doomed to disaster too, but what choice did he have, when she was already increasing? He lost Caroline when he tried to seduce Owen, who was by then married to Tom's brother.

If Owen had agreed, he'd have abandoned him anyway. He didn't love Owen and never had. Tom had all but heard a clock ticking, though, measuring out the time before his marriage went to hell, cursed by a goddess whose commands had been laid upon him in the womb. Commands he had disregarded at best and spat upon at worst.

But if he'd run away with Owen, even briefly, the goddess would have had no reason to punish Caroline or her child, would she? For months, Tom had burst awake in the middle of the night, soaked in sweat and with tears streaming down his face. The dreams were always the same in essence, though the horrific details varied. Their child stillborn, blue and pitiful, with Caroline's face set in a rictus of grief; Caroline screaming in agony as she bled to death in labor, both she and their child gone in a moment. Death after death, horror upon horror, and all of it because of Tom's cowardice and shame.

Tom had no way out. Caroline would never leave him without cause and make her baby fatherless. She had an innate sense of right that had never wavered, to his knowledge, except in that one lapse in judgment that led to their son's conception. He had no way to save them all from the catastrophe of his own creation except by creating another catastrophe. At least that solution played to his strengths. In the end, he had been thrown from the house, with Caroline and the child left safely under the aegis of her brother-in-law Owen's blessing — not the result he'd expected, but a positive outcome for the two of them, at least.

And now here he was, embroiled in yet another engagement. And about to be married that evening — if he could only think of how to dress. A candle. He would need a candle. Tom pushed shakily away from the nightstand and felt his way to the fireplace, tripping over something and striking his forehead against the mantelpiece. He caught the edge of it with his fingers and leaned there, panting. The bruise might be difficult to explain, particularly if Leighton dragged him into the temple half-dressed and apparently unwilling.

That thought was enough to tip Tom into hysteria; he slumped there, laughing and laughing and laughing, shaking with it. The door slammed open. Leighton took him by the shoulders and shouted at him, Tom didn't even know what. Tears streamed down his face and his belly hurt. He was still laughing, or sobbing, or perhaps both.

He couldn't stop as Leighton maneuvered him about the room, pushing him into a chair and getting his feet into boots, cursing as Tom went limp. Then he was on his feet, and his arms were going into coat sleeves. He batted at Leighton's hands as the man tried to tie his cravat, earning himself a new stream of muttered curses.

Tom roused a little as they stumbled down the stairs, Leighton's arm firm around his waist, and he blinked as they emerged into the misty evening with the housemaid's worried-sounding questions echoing behind them.

He looked down at himself and automatically smoothed the fabric of his coat. It was the green one, not the blue one that flattered his eyes. "I don't think this is the one I'd have chosen to be married in," he mumbled.

"And I think I made it clear you're not making decisions any longer." Leighton let out an unpleasant bark of laughter. "Trust you to give a damn for your bloody coat, when you've been carrying on like a mute madman for hours."

It took Tom a moment to understand the assessment of his character contained in that. When he did, he jerked away from Leighton's hold, stumbling a little but righting himself on his own. Leighton simply watched him stagger and reel like a drunkard, his lip curled in contempt, dark eyes cold. The numbness Tom had been fighting seeped back in, as insidious as any poison. What did it matter, anyway? Leighton thought him worthless. But then again, so did everyone else Tom had ever known.

They stared at one another for a long moment. A pressure built in Tom's chest, enough that he thought he might burst open from it, spill his heart and entrails on the damp-streaked pavement at Leighton's feet. Leighton's brow furrowed; he opened his mouth.

And he turned away abruptly as the rumble of carriage wheels and the clopping of hooves echoed down the narrow street. Whatever he might have said was gone forever.

A smart, glossy dark blue coach drawn by four magnificent bays appeared out of the mist and pulled to a stop; a stout middle-aged man in sober black hopped spryly down from the box where he had been perching beside the coachman.

"Sir," he said, with a bow to Leighton. "Everything you require is packed and ready."

"Good." Leighton nodded. "We'll go to Mirreith's temple first, and then on to Maberley. Oh, and Preston," he went on, in the tone of one just remembering a trivial detail, "this is Mr. Drake, my intended."

Preston stared at him, and Tom felt the back of his neck heat and his cheeks flush. Leighton had just relegated him to a status lower than that of a servant by presenting him to Preston, rather than the other way around. It was a calculated insult. It was designed to put Tom in his place. And all at once, it was impossible to bear. Perhaps he deserved it in some greater sense, but he had not earned it from Leighton.

"Or not," Tom said.

Leighton froze, arrested in the motion of walking to the carriage, his shoulders rigid with tension. For a moment Tom felt he had stepped into a tableau — The Recalcitrant Bridegroom, posed after dinner for the enjoyment of the guests. One of the horses snorted and shifted his hooves, and the spell broke.

"What did you just say?" Leighton turned slowly and

fixed his unblinking gaze on Tom. The force in that look nearly had Tom stumbling back. Leighton's expression was quite blank, but he could have committed murder in that moment, Tom had no doubt. Leighton took one step forward. "What did you just say to me."

Tom held his ground. He had nowhere to go, and nothing to lose, and if Leighton strangled him here in the street it would matter to no one, least of all to him. He vaguely noticed that Preston showed rather more intelligence, and vanished around the side of the carriage as if by magic.

"I wasn't necessarily speaking to you," Tom said, with just the slightest betraying quaver. "You chose to address yourself to your valet when you should have spoken to me. Perhaps I chose to do the same."

"He's my butler, not my valet. And furthermore —"

"Oh, I beg your pardon!" Tom's voice rose, sending muffled echoes back from the houses looming overhead. "I should have realized. Of course I'm to occupy a position higher than that of your valet in the household, but I couldn't possibly expect to rank above the bloody *butler*."

He almost shouted those last words; they rang in his ears, joining the buzzing of his brain and the sick pounding of blood through his every vein and artery.

"Drake," Leighton said, his tone icy. It sent a shiver down Tom's back. "I have had enough. More than enough. I found you all but catatonic, you laughed and wept like a madman while I dressed you like a child, and now you're screaming like a fishwife in the street. Get in the carriage before I drag you there."

"No," Tom cried. "No, I will not get in the carriage,

and I'm not going to marry you, not if you treat me like —"

"Like what?" It was Leighton's turn to shout. It rang through the street and startled the horses, who pranced and whinnied as the coachman cursed. "Like the whore you so readily agreed to be? You've spent my banknotes on frippery and wine for weeks, and now you want to get out of the bargain because you don't think I'm treating you with sufficient fucking respect?"

Faster than Tom could follow, Leighton was right there, looming over him far more threateningly than his two inches of advantage in height should have allowed.

"You're the one who offered me your arse for a few guineas," Leighton hissed, his eyes blazing. "And I'm damn well going to get what I've paid for. So get in the carriage."

"Go to *hell*," Tom spat. He shoved Leighton in the chest; Leighton caught him by the wrists and used their momentum to drag them together, Tom's arms caught and pinned between them. "You pretend to care about your precious cousin, when all you are is a selfish, whoremongering, blackmailing bastard —"

Leighton descended like lightning. He savaged Tom's mouth with lips and teeth and tongue, drove every thought from his mind and stifled every word in his throat. Arousal flowed like brandy through his veins and sang in every nerve. Leighton's powerful grasp on his arms hurt in the best possible way, every point of bruising contact a reassurance that Leighton had him, and wouldn't let him go. Tom knew he ought to resist — distantly, he knew it. Instead every limb went lax, and he swayed into Leighton's hold like a drowning man clinging to his rescuer. He had held himself up for so long, treading water and sinking a little more all the time. Perhaps he'd drag them both down to the darkness. But if he did, it wouldn't be his responsibility — it would be Leighton's.

The kiss went on and on and gentled at last, Leighton's tongue moving lazily around his own and mapping every contour of his mouth.

When Leighton lifted his head, it took Tom a moment to blink his eyes open. Leighton filled his vision, blotting out the rest of the world: just dark eyes, a reddened mouth, and black hair mussed by the chill breeze from off the nearby river. Tom's back was cold, but in front he could feel nothing but the heat of Leighton's body and the pressure of his long, clever fingers around Tom's wrists.

"Get in the carriage, Tom," Leighton said, a whisper against Tom's lips that he felt as much as heard. Leighton's breath was hot too, and sweet, and the space between them had filled with the scent of Leighton's subtle cologne and of their desire. "I'm not asking."

Tom couldn't speak — he could hardly form a coherent thought. Leighton had him, and Tom had no more fight left in him. He surrendered, welcoming the floating sensation of giving up the battle. He managed a slight nod, and Leighton wrapped an arm around his waist and led him to the coach.

Chapter Six

THE BREAKFAST PARLOR AT MABERLEY was one of Mal's favorite rooms. It had a pleasant aspect, with large windows offering a view down the hill on which the house sat. A small lake spread out at the bottom of the hill, and right then it was lit in streaks of pink and silver from the newly-risen sun. Will had always been an early riser, and even now, when his illness kept him abed nearly constantly, the servants kept to his preferences and filled the sideboard with fresh bread and eggs and bacon as soon as the sun was up.

Like Mal, they stubbornly refused to admit the inevitable. Mal loved and hated it in equal measure — the futility of it agonizing, but their loyalty impossible to discourage. How many mornings had he sat here with Will, laughing over their coffee, planning the day's business or amusements with equal pleasure in either, simply because they were together? Mal had few friends, and even fewer he'd consider intimate. Will was more than his cousin, more than his heir. He was Mal's brother in every way that mattered.

Mal turned away from the windows with a curse and ran his hands through his hair. The movement was nearly enough to make him lose his balance; a night without sleep had left him lightheaded.

Tom was upstairs, presumably still sleeping more deeply than he deserved. His husband. Thomas Drake-Leighton as of the night before, bound to him in a ceremony overseen by a tight-lipped priestess who had accepted Mal's offering of three hundred guineas but given little enough warmth or pleasantries in return.

After the marriage rites, Tom went mutely back to the carriage like a sleepwalker. He hadn't spoken a single word on the journey, when they arrived at Maberley, or when Mal sent him up to his room with a footman to show him the way.

For a moment Mal considered following him and taking what was his due. He knew damn well Tom wouldn't put up a fight. Tired and worn, he simply didn't have it in him. And it was more than that, too, something that went deeper than mere exhaustion. When Mal kissed him, Tom had all but gone limp in his hold — arousing in other circumstances, but under those, unsettling. His eyes were blank when they opened, their blue as clear and lovely as ever but lacking that lively spark that made Tom the vitally attractive man he was.

Some base part of Mal wanted to take him even so. Strip him, maneuver him however he wanted, and use him without care. He would have had complete control; he could have done anything.

The flare of desperate lust when he imagined it brought on an even stronger wave of nausea. Mal longed for Tom's submission, for him to yield. But taking him the night before would have been nothing short of rape.

Mal fled to the library instead. He locked himself in, and then he paced the night away, unfit even to look in on

Will. Tom was clearly suffering some malady of the mind or the heart. Forcing him into this marriage, and in such a way, probably made Mal a monster. He knew it; likely Tom knew it. He couldn't stand the thought of allowing Will to see it too. And he would have — he knew Mal far too well to miss the war raging within him between his better self and the part of him that would destroy Tom utterly just because he could.

A neglected cup of coffee sat on the table — to the right of the top, of course. Even though Mal was the head of the family, this was Will's home. The empty place setting before Will's seat was all Mal could see. He took up his cup and sipped at it, hardly caring that it was cold. He needed something to buck him up. At any moment Will would wake, and send for him, and then the explanations would begin.

Because Mal, coward that he was, had not yet apprised Will of his plan to save his life.

MORNINGS WERE NEVER KIND to Tom. It was true that he often overindulged, but even when he'd remained as sober as a high priest the night before he woke slowly and with difficulty, blinking and cursing and fumbling about until someone pressed a cup of coffee into his hand.

That morning, Tom sprang bolt upright in bed with his heart racing and panic pressing in on his mind from all directions. Cold sweat bathed his face and chest and dampened the shirt and drawers he'd worn to sleep. His whole body felt horridly clammy, and his hands shook as he raised them to push the moist tendrils of hair off his forehead.

Maberley. He was in a bedroom at William Leighton's estate, and last night he'd married Malcolm Leighton. Tom had to repeat it a few times, in his mind and then in a rough whisper he hardly recognized as his own, before the reality of it set in.

The faintest light of dawn filtered through gaps in the heavy blue drapes covering the windows to the left of the bed. It showed Tom a perfectly, reassuringly mundane room, the rug patterned with pale blue roses and the wardrobe and washstand freshly polished and gleaming. A gilt clock ticked away on the mantel. It was just ten minutes to seven — at least three hours before Tom usually rose. The night before felt like a dream from which he couldn't quite awaken. His sluggish mind and the heaviness of his limbs were more than his typical morning lassitude; he didn't even want a cup of coffee, or a bath, or anything else.

Tom lay back on his pillows, flipping the top one over to hide the damp left behind by his perspiration. At least the strange despairing malaise that had taken him last night had partially passed. What had he been thinking when he fell into Leighton's arms like that? The divorce had hit him hard, the news of his son's birth shocking even in its inevitability. That had to account for it. He squirmed a little, mortification seeping in around the haze of emotion that left his memories of the night before so foggy. It hardly mattered. It wouldn't happen again, because he assuredly didn't *want* it to happen again.

It could all be forgotten, pushed aside. He had never yielded to Leighton's masterful hands and voice, the skill and passion of his kiss…Tom had a lifetime of practice in ignoring what he didn't want to remember. He could sleep again. The hush of the house nearly ensured it. He closed his eyes.

Someone moaned, long and sharp and filled with pain.

Tom's heart nearly jumped out of his chest again, and his eyelids popped open. He listened for a long moment, straining to hear more than his own panting breaths.

Whoever it was cried out again, lower this time, more of a drawn-out sob. Tom shoved the bedclothes away and set his feet on the floor, gripping the edge of the mattress as the world seemed to shift around him.

When he rocked to his feet and peered about the room, he discovered his clothes had vanished. No doubt the footman who'd brought him upstairs — the man's name had vanished into the same obscurity that had absorbed most of the night before — had helpfully taken them to be pressed. But Tom could hardly wander the house as he was now. With little hope of finding anything, he opened the wardrobe, and was pleasantly surprised to see a dressing gown on a hook at the side. It was a little too long, but so much the better as he had no breeches.

The dressing gown securely belted about his waist, he cracked the door open and peered into the corridor. He ought to be able to find the source of the noise. Maberley was a fair-sized house, or so it had seemed from his brief glimpse of it in the dark as he left the carriage, but it wasn't a great estate. And those cries of pain had sounded quite near.

Tom cocked his head and listened. To his right, the corridor extended ten yards or so, with a door on either side. It ended in a dormer window that let in enough grayish light to illuminate that end, but to the left the dimness was nearly impenetrable. Another faint moan broke the stillness. It seemed to be coming from the right, so Tom eased through the door, heart spiking as he overbalanced and almost slammed it, and weaved his way toward the window.

When he'd heard it in his bedchamber, the voice had seemed more distant than it would have if coming just from next door, so Tom crossed to the door opposite and paused to listen again. There was a faint rustle, a sigh, and then another muffled sob. He stood paralyzed with indecision. The corridor was quite empty, and if William — for it had to be William in the room before him — had rung the bell, surely someone must be coming to see to him. But no one came, and William groaned again, and Tom could hardly leave the poor fellow to suffer when he might be in need of assistance.

He tapped once, lightly, and then turned the knob and swung the door lightly open.

Where Tom's bedchamber was sparse, elegant, and airy, with the faint scent of lemon oil, William's was close and too warm, redolent with sickness and laudanum and the bitter reek of pain. Bile rose to the back of Tom's throat. He wanted nothing more than to turn tail and run. Death seemed to hover so closely in this stuffy space, near enough to sweep his cloak over anyone who entered and bear them off indiscriminately.

A slight gasp from the bed drew him back from his morbid imagination to the man enduring all of this. Tom could leave the room; William could not. His courage rose with his pity and horror, and he stepped inside.

"I beg your pardon," he said softly. "I heard you call out."

The bed had probably been moved to be closer to the fireplace on the left end of the room, for it was near enough to have only a chair in between, and the other end of the room had been taken up with a cot for a nurse or servant and an odd clutter of tables bearing bottles and vials and medical implements Tom was quite glad he couldn't identify. The door opened just opposite the foot of the bed, and all Tom could see was a mound of blankets.

The pile of bedclothes shifted as Tom spoke, and a faint voice replied, "Is that you, Carter?"

The draft of cold air around his ankles reminded Tom to close the door before he stepped around the bed. "No, it's not Carter. It's Tom Drake, do you remember me from school? I arrived last night with Leighton."

Glittering eyes peered out at him from a wasted face, and Tom could only stare for a moment, any other words faded from his mind. He would never have recognized the merry William in this wretched, miserable wraith of a man. Good goddess. If this was what Leighton had always in his mind, his desperation was hardly surprising. If this had been Arthur — Tom shivered.

"I'm sorry to intrude. I didn't hear anyone coming to look in on you, and you sounded like you were dy—" Bloody fucking hell. Tom forced a cough to cover his error and hoped William couldn't see the hot, mortified flush that swept his face. "Pardon me. You sounded as if you needed assistance."

Shockingly, William's pale, chapped lips curved in a smile. "It's all right," he whispered, and then he coughed quite genuinely, a horrid, wet sound that went on and on and ended in a choking whimper. Tom dashed forward and then stopped, hovering too close for politeness but having no idea what to do.

He looked wildly about him, found the bell rope by the bedpost, and gave it a violent tug, and then another for good measure. Damn William's servants, were they all lounging in bed while their master coughed up his lungs?

At last the coughing fit subsided. "William," he said, urgently, "I rang the bell, I'm sure someone will be here any moment—"

"Carter went to fetch hot water," William rasped. "He'll be back soon." He fell back against his pillows and his eyes fluttered shut.

Tom had only once before felt so terribly helpless, during those awful months when he watched Caroline grow with their child and knew he would be the ruin of both of them. Before, he had tried to save them by leaving them as far behind as possible. Now he was supposed to somehow use his blessing to save this man, a man Leighton loved far more than Tom had ever loved his wife. And he couldn't even manage to assist him when he coughed, only stood there like a fool and probably made it worse with his interference.

"I am dying, you know," William said, and Tom jumped.

"Oh, come now, don't say that," he tried. It rang horribly false. "You'll pull through. You Leightons are like rats. Survive anywhere. You survived Harrow."

Tom knew his pitiful attempt at bucking-up deserved only scorn, but William, being the same kind fellow he'd been at their dreadful school, managed another faint smile. "I won't survive this, though. So when you said it sounded like—" William paused, drew a rasping breath, and went on, "—like I'm dying. It's all right. I don't mind. I rather wish someone would — would say it aloud."

Tom bit his lip. What gave a man the strength to speak so, in the face of his own agonizing, drawn-out mortality? He knew he would never find it in himself.

After a long moment, William's eyes blinked open slowly. They were still the same vivid green Tom remembered from school, heartbreakingly lovely amidst the ruin of his other features. "I've always so much laudanum in me," he said slowly. "I never quite know what's real. But you are Tom Drake, aren't you? What are you doing here? Or am I conversing with the curtains again?"

That startled a laugh out of Tom, and drew an answering chuckle from William that ended in another cough. Thankfully it was just the one, and not another fit.

"I'm really Tom Drake. Not a curtain, I assure you." He had already said he arrived last night with Leighton, hadn't he? It seemed cruel to remind William of his own lapse, but he could hardly avoid it. "I'm your guest for the nonce, it seems. Leighton and I —" He stopped again, suddenly aghast with realization. William didn't know. He *couldn't* know Leighton had meant to marry him, or he'd have expected Tom's presence at Maberley.

"Yes of course," William said, sounding apologetic. "You did say a moment ago. Didn't know the two of you were friends. But," and he paused for a few labored breaths, a fluid rasp echoing beneath, "very glad to have you, hope you'll stay a while."

Tom was left at a loss for what to reply, and William seemed to be lapsing into unconsciousness, his eyelids drooping and his head lolling. Footsteps in the corridor were perhaps the most welcome sound Tom had ever heard.

He turned back to the door just in time to see Leighton burst through. He was in his shirtsleeves, his hair mussed and his eyes bloodshot and shadowed.

"What the devil are you doing here?" He didn't pause for an answer, only shoved Tom aside and careened around the bed to get to William. A young man bearing a teapot on a tray, presumably Carter, came in behind him and hurried to set his burden on one of the tables, immediately pouring a cup and beginning to dose it with drops of liquid from one of the many vials. Leighton took William's hand, gently chafing his wrist and murmuring to him. Tom's heart gave a painful squeeze. That kind of love, whole-hearted and devoted — he had never known it, and he never would.

Tom slipped out the door unnoticed and unwanted and made his way back to his bedchamber alone.

Chapter Seven

"Tom?" Mal knocked softly, though his impatience was mounting. He needed to see Tom now, at once, before he could leave his bedchamber and speak to anyone. Thank the gods he hadn't had time to say much to Will, but Mal knew his kind-hearted cousin would want to see Tom as soon as he had the strength for it. Mal had to speak to him first.

Mal raised his hand to knock again, but hesitated. Will had only just lapsed into exhausted slumber after hours of restless misery. He couldn't risk waking him. "Tom?" he said, just above a whisper. "Are you in there?"

Not a sound came through the door. Mal tried the knob, a little surprised to find it unlocked, and slipped within. For a moment he thought the room was empty, but then he saw Tom slumped in a chair by the cold fireplace, still in that absurd too-large dressing gown and utterly still. His eyes were open and fixed on the fireplace, but Mal doubted he really saw the pile of ashes on the hearth.

The curtains were still drawn, and the bedchamber felt chill and empty, with none of the sense of life human habitation usually brought to a space.

"Tom, what are you doing?" Mal's voice rang sharply in the stillness, and he winced. It was quite absurd to feel like an intruder. This was Will's house, all but his own.

Tom was the one who had no real place here. And Tom was his husband. Mal had every right to enter his bedchamber whenever he wished, did he not?

Mal pushed down the twinge of discomfort that thought produced and strode boldly across the room to stand directly in front of Tom. The man didn't so much as twitch. "Tom!" he said, with more force. "What the devil?"

Tom's eyes flicked up for a moment, he sighed, and then he returned to his blank contemplation of the hearth. This was far too much like Tom's fugue of the night before. Then, Mal's anger and his terror for Will had taken him over completely, eradicating the impulses of concern and tenderness that had almost come to the fore. This morning, after no sleep and hours spent soothing Will's pain and comforting him through his feverish ramblings, he hadn't the strength for anger. Sand poured in his eyes and a beating administered to his every limb would have been an improvement over his current condition.

Mal yielded to compassion and to simple gravity and went to one knee beside Tom's chair. He could see his face more clearly now, the faint tracks of tears on his pale cheeks and the downturn of his lips.

It occurred to Mal for the first time that perhaps Tom wasn't quite so callous as he appeared, and as his reputation had painted him. Mal had been so obsessed with the idea of saving Will that he'd only seen the divorce decree as the last piece of his plan; he hadn't stopped to consider that it could only have been issued if Tom's wife had given birth to their child, and then cut Tom loose immediately after. Any man might be struck down by shock and grief and a whole poisonous brew of complicated feelings. The realization hit Mal like a thunderbolt, and burning shame came rushing in on its heels. Gods, but he was a bastard. A cruel, thoughtless, selfish bastard.

A child. Tom had a child, and Mal hadn't even thought to ask if he had a son or a daughter.

Words seemed inadequate — any of the words Mal could bring to mind, anyway. Instead he reached out and gently took Tom's hand, wrapping his own around it and stroking the underside of Tom's wrist with his thumb.

Slowly, the soft skin beneath his fingers began to warm, and Tom let out a long breath. He shifted at last and looked down at their joined hands, his brows drawing together in something like bewilderment.

"What are you doing?" His rusty voice sounded as if he hadn't used it in years and had all but forgotten how.

Mal swallowed. What was he doing? Giving comfort had never been one of his strengths. Will had teased him once that he was as useful in a sickroom as any other large, clumsy animal, and Mal hadn't argued. He felt just as helpless now. Anything he said would be wrong, he knew it: cold, or awkward, or unkind, whether he meant it or not.

But he needed to do something. Tom had no one — no one but Mal, who'd married him for reasons entirely unrelated to affection or liking or even desire, much as Mal did desire him. Perhaps Tom deserved his current state of friendlessness. Even so. Mal had promised the night before to keep and protect him, to stand with him and honor him.

Mal leaned in, slowly enough that Tom could pull away if he wished, and set his lips gently against Tom's mouth. He tried to give rather than take, coax Tom's plush lips to part rather than demand entrance; he teased the seam with his tongue and dipped within for the slightest, most tantalizing taste. His heart sped up just at that little contact. Tom was sweet, his lips as cold as the rest of him from sitting so long in an unheated room, but the inside of his mouth was like warm honey.

Gods, but he *wanted*. Wanted to seize Tom, crush him in his arms, throw him down on the bed and make him moan — but not yet. Not until Tom understood that it would be an act of more than simple dominance and lust.

Mal hadn't even understood himself that it would be more than that, until that very moment. He broke the kiss and sat back, breathing like a bellows. Good gods. How had Tom gotten under his skin? It was lust, and guilt, and the feelings stirred up by Will's illness and his own exhaustion. It could not possibly be more.

Tom blinked at him, his lips parted. The kiss had brought a little color back to his cheeks, just a faint peony flush on his perfect cheekbones. He was beautiful, a sacramental painting brought to life.

"Leighton? What is this? Is William all right?" Tom's hesitance near broke Mal's heart, and his concern for Will filled it with a twisting, painful joy that he did not at all want to examine.

"He's asleep." Mal cleared his throat and pressed Tom's hand. If Tom chose to ignore the kiss, Mal would be more than happy to do the same. "You're chilled to the bone, Tom. Why don't you have a fire?"

Tom's eyes cleared, and he looked about him with a little more alertness. "What — the light's different," he said slowly. "I thought I'd only just sat down."

"It's been hours. You left Will's room hours ago. He was glad to see you, by the by. I think it cheered him to have a houseguest."

A faint smile lit Tom's face. "I'm glad of it." The smile died away. "He's so very ill, Leighton. I didn't know."

"You didn't know?" Annoyance flared up again, though Mal tried hard to tamp it down. Was Tom really so self-centered? Did he never listen to a word out of Mal's mouth, for the gods' sakes? "How could you not? I told you again and again. Why else would I have been so desperate to marry you?"

With a violent tug, Tom pulled his hand away and stood, knocking into Mal's shoulder so roughly that he fell back on his arse with a thump.

"Why else indeed?" Tom tugged the dressing gown more tightly about him and wrapped his arms around his torso. He hunched in on himself, his head hanging down. "Go and sleep while you can."

Mal stared up at him, too stunned by his own tactlessness even to care about his less than dignified position. Oh, good *gods*. "Tom, that's not what I meant. I meant only that —"

"I know what you meant." Defeat bled through every word. "I know. William is everything to you. He should be. He's a decent fellow, always was. He deserves better than this, and I don't blame you for being willing to do — anything, no matter how much you hate it." He let out an ugly little laugh. "I don't blame you."

"I blame myself." Could he do or say nothing right when it came to Tom? Must he always be hurting him? He shouldn't care. Tom should be nothing to him. But he did blame himself, so bitterly the words tasted like ashes. He pushed off the floor, every joint creaking, and moved to stand by Tom. "I didn't mean it like that. I give you my word I didn't."

Tom looked up at him, shaking his overlong hair out of his face as he did so. He'd always been so particular about his appearance, even at school. When had he stopped making the effort to be always fashionable, always perfect? Mal would have said that Tom's vanity was one of his more irritating foibles, but now it troubled him that Tom didn't seem to care. Perhaps he had stopped caring when he agreed to marry Mal, and he no longer had a reason to attract anyone. That thought bothered Mal more than anything.

"You're not ashamed of marrying me, then?" Warning bells rang in Mal's mind. Nothing good could lie behind a question asked in such a mild tone of voice.

"Of course I'm not ashamed." And he wasn't, not precisely. It wasn't a lie. He was ashamed of marrying under such circumstances, ashamed of his own behavior, and not precisely thrilled to have married such a notorious rake. "Of course I'm not," he repeated, with firmness.

Tom's expression hardened, his eyes going as sharp as flint. "Odd that you should say so. William asked me this morning why I was in his house, and said he had no idea we were friends."

"What was I supposed to say to him? That I was marrying to save his life? He'd have been horrified."

"At least that's honest," Tom spat, his face twisted with rage and humiliation. He paced away from Mal, hands working in the silk of the dressing gown and knuckles white. "You could at least pretend he'd be grateful rather than disgusted."

"Not by you — dammit, Tom, stop twisting every word out of my mouth! He'd hate the thought of me, and of you, doing something he'd see as hopeless anyway, just for his sake." Mal stopped, breathing hard, and tried to bring his temper back under control. He'd been all but shouting. "He likes you. He's — oh, hell. That's why I came to find you. He's happy for us."

Tom's eyes went wide and his mouth dropped open. He should have looked ridiculous, but Mal only wanted to kiss him all the more. What was the *matter* with him?

"I beg your pardon?" Tom asked bewilderedly. Mal saw the moment realization dawned. Very slowly, as if speaking to an idiot, Tom said, "What did you tell him, Leighton?"

Mal rubbed his hands over his face and then dropped his arms by his sides. There was really no point in hiding. "I told him we were married."

"And?" Tom crossed his arms and cocked his head.

"And then." Mal stared down at the floor, feeling like both an idiot and a coward — understandable, since he was both. "And then he smiled like I haven't seen him smile in months, and he congratulated me, and he wished us both very happy." He'd also teased Mal about how much in love he must be, by the soppy way he said Tom's name — and that detail Mal would keep to himself, even under torture.

"Happy," Tom stated flatly. "Really. I suppose this is not the part where you disabused him of any such absurd notion?"

"What would you have had me do? He's worn to a shadow. You saw for yourself. A shock could kill him, but hope — hope can keep a man alive even when his body can hardly function." Mal stepped toward Tom again, drawn by the impulse to persuade him, and by the simple desire to be nearer. "We must pretend for his sake."

"Pretend to what? Goddess, you want me to pretend to be *in love* with you?" Tom shook his head and laughed. "If I had that sort of talent for dissimulation, I'd be on the stage."

That hit home, like a knife between his ribs. It took every ounce of self-control Mal possessed not to double over from the blow. He didn't give a damn if Tom loved him, or could ever love him. It had to be his pride that ached like that. Anger rose up, a welcome relief from his confusion, from the softer impulses that made him weak. So much for showing Tom kindness, for feeling sympathy. He would treat him as he deserved.

"Then you can only imagine how difficult it will be for me," Mal said, cold and hard, every word as pointed as an arrow and launched with the same precision. "You at least have the advantage of playing the whore for every man you meet, and half the women. This ought to be child's play for you. But I'll need to feign affection for the laughingstock of every society drawing room." He forced a laugh. "I'll need to be convincing indeed when not even your own wife could keep up the pretense of loving you long enough to bear your child."

If Mal had been allowing himself to feel, he might have wanted to weep at the change that came over Tom as he spoke. With each word, a little more of Tom's bravado chipped away: a flash of pain in his bright blue eyes, then a dulling of their light, a contraction of the shoulders and compression of those soft lips.

The silence grew until the room fairly throbbed with it. Tom stood as if he had been turned to stone, all the life and warmth bled out of him. "Very well," he said abruptly, with no inflection at all. Mal clenched his fists. It was either that or reach out for him and pull him close. "We'll play the happy lovers for William and his household."

Mal opened his mouth to reply, but Tom held up a hand to silence him. "On one condition, and if you don't fulfill it, I'll tell William the truth myself." Mal could only nod. He knew as well as Tom did, the bastard, that Mal would agree to anything to keep Will as calm and cheerful as could be managed. "You'll stay the hell away from me," Tom grated out. "You won't enter this room. You won't speak to me unless it's necessary, and certainly not when there aren't others present. And if you put your fucking mouth on me again you'll regret it."

Mal thought he'd probably win that fight, but he knew that wasn't the best parting shot to take.

"I already do." He turned away quickly, but not quite quickly enough to miss the ripple of pure humiliated misery that passed over Tom's expressive face. Getting the last word was not nearly as satisfying as he had hoped.

Chapter Eight

WILLIAM DIDN'T RECOVER. His condition didn't improve in even the slightest degree, and Leighton grew darker and more volatile by the day.

Tom stayed as far out of his way as possible, and Leighton kept his promise — he came nowhere near Tom whenever he had the choice, seeing him only at dinner and on the few brief visits they made to William's sickroom together. But as his frustration edged into despair, his mood seemed to infect everyone in the house, from the housemaids who slunk about their duties in despondent silence to Tom himself, who hadn't been precisely filled with cheer to begin with.

As often as he could, Tom left the house and explored the grounds, taking endlessly long walks around the lake and riding out through the woods that bounded the estate. The weather made such expeditions utterly miserable, varying from freezing rain to rain that wasn't quite freezing, with very brief detours into lowering overcast and biting winds, but it was still far more pleasant than the atmosphere inside Maberley.

Tom handed his overcoat to a footman as he returned from one such walk a week after the wedding. Water dribbled down his neck from his hair in icy rivulets, reminding him how long he'd gone without a proper cut.

He'd forgone a hat, since the wind would have carried it off in seconds anyhow.

"Was that Dr. Porter's carriage I saw in the drive an hour gone?" he asked, stamping the mud from his boots on the oilcloth that lay by the front door. It was hopeless; he bent and began to tug them off.

"Yes, sir," the man said. Henry? Tom thought that might be his name. He'd spent precious little time getting to know anyone who lived here, and they seemed as willing to avoid him. "And he went in to see Mr. Leighton after he left Mr. William. I haven't heard a peep from him since."

Henry sent a quick, nervous glance at the closed door to the library, where Leighton spent nearly every moment he wasn't at William's bedside, as far as Tom could tell. He must have been finding the time to bathe and change his clothing, since he never appeared less than respectably turned out, but when, where, or if he slept was anyone's guess. The footmen had to tiptoe in to replenish the brandy decanter and replace the glasses on the sideboard, but Tom thought they drew straws each morning to determine who would place himself in the line of fire.

"Do you know what —" Tom stopped himself. He was Leighton's husband, after all. They might spend little enough time together, but questioning a footman as to the doctor's conversation with Leighton would end any chance they had of pretending to be married in more than name. "Never mind. Thank you, Henry."

Henry nodded, hopefully because that was actually his name, and took Tom's coat and boots away to be cleaned. He moved past the library door with exaggerated care, as if terrified to draw Leighton's attention. Tom frowned. This had gone far enough. The servants had not to his knowledge abated their care of their ill master as yet, but it was only a matter of time before the house came tumbling down around their ears.

The sensation of responsibility sat uncomfortably on Tom's shoulders. No one but he could possibly intervene — but goddess, how hopeless did matters need to be for *Tom* to be the one taking charge? No one with any sense would entrust him with organizing a card party, let alone this.

He crossed the hall to the library door and stood listening a moment. Nothing, not so much as a whisper or the rustle of a newspaper. The whole house felt as if it had fallen under the spell of some malicious fairy, hushed and brooding; Tom could almost imagine that he was the only animated inhabitant, all the others frozen into some unhealthy enchanted slumber. Even the furnishings seemed to be withering under the strain. The grandfather clock against the wall ticked more slowly than it should, and the dried flowers in the vase on the small table near the door were drooping and dusty.

Tom set his hand on the doorknob and forced himself to turn it. Goddess, but he had no desire to confront Leighton. Still, it had to be done. He had hoped, prayed even, that Dr. Porter would have had some good news — that the miracle Leighton longed for had materialized. It wasn't impossible that it could have been delayed a little. Even a goddess might need a few days to bring one about, and surely she had other calls on her time and attention.

But clearly no such miracle had occurred, and they

were running out of time.

The door clicked to behind him, and Tom looked about the library with some curiosity. He'd only set foot in it once during his stay, and that for merely a moment. He'd thought to make it his own haven in the house, since reading was the only sedentary occupation he enjoyed, but he'd withdrawn the moment he saw Leighton pacing by the window, brandy glass in hand.

It was a lovely room, really, far too pleasant for its current occupant and his cares. Tall windows nearly the height of the room looked out on the eastern end of the lake where it curved around the house, and whoever had furnished the room had clearly done so with care and at great expense. Deep, comfortable chairs upholstered in leather, small tables for holding a book and a glass, long, polished tables for spreading out many books at once, and several sofas perfect for napping were spread around the room in just the right positions to catch the natural light. All of the bookshelves were toward the back in rows to keep them out of the sun.

It took Tom a moment to find Leighton amidst all the furnishings, but he spotted him at last, sprawled on one of the sofas nearest the bookcases. He was fast asleep, one arm dangling over the side of the sofa and the other flung above his head.

He was in his shirtsleeves, his coat draped over him as a makeshift blanket and his booted feet resting carelessly on an embroidered cushion at the end of the sofa. Tom's gut gave an uncomfortable twinge of sympathy at the sight. Damn it all, but Leighton had no right to make Tom *feel*. He'd made it abundantly clear how little he thought of

Tom, how much he despised him. Leighton's parting words from their conversation the day after their marriage still rang in Tom's ears, haunting him as he rode or walked or ran, desperate to escape the cruel truth of them.

Caroline hadn't waited a moment to be shot of him. His own brother had cast him out — and for good reason, but that wound still ached, like a bullet buried deep inside him that the surgeon couldn't remove. He would probably never see his own son.

And Leighton thought they were all quite right to want nothing to do with him. Thought him worthless. He'd had one use, his blessing, and he'd failed even in simply standing there and following the goddess's supposed plan for him.

But Tom still couldn't look at Leighton, exposed and vulnerable as he was now, without compassion. The inky shadows beneath Leighton's eyes stood out starkly black against his waxy, ashen skin, and he frowned even in his sleep, brows furrowed and lips twisted. He suffered because he loved, and Tom could only respect him for it. No one in his own family would sit this kind of vigil for him, were he in William's place. His own father had told him early and often how he wished Tom had died at birth, taking what the elder Drake saw as the shame of Mirreith's mark with him out of the world. To him, any man who yielded to another was as worthless as a woman — more so, since at least women could bear children, their only use in Tom's father's view.

"No son of mine will be some other man's catamite," he'd shouted at Tom during one of his many rages. That one had been precipitated by Tom's return from school bearing a black eye and a letter from the headmaster recounting Tom's tears when it was inflicted. "You'll do your duty by this family and be a man, or I'll cast you out to starve." Tom had been eight years old.

No, none of the Drakes would give a damn if Tom lay dying; at least his father was already in hell and wouldn't be there to celebrate. It was rather dreadful, but he envied William his situation. He might be enduring an agonizing, lingering death, but Tom would take that and gladly if it meant someone might weep for him when it was over.

Tom crept a little closer, silent in his stocking feet. Leighton didn't stir. If he hadn't been able to see Leighton's chest rising and falling slightly, Tom might have thought him a corpse. He certainly had the complexion of one.

How long had it been since Leighton slept? Tom needed to speak with him, but he was willing enough to use the excuse of Leighton's exhaustion to wait a few hours. A few steps closer, and Tom could see faint marks on Leighton's cheeks: the tracks of tears. Tom's heart stopped for a moment. He wouldn't have imagined Leighton capable of weeping; he was just the sort of man Tom's father would have approved of, strong and steady and stoic in the face of anything.

Apparently even Leighton had his breaking point, and had cried himself to sleep on the library sofa — just as Tom had done nearly twenty years before after searching out the word *catamite* in a dictionary.

Tom stared, fighting the warring impulses Leighton stirred in his breast. He wanted to find a shawl or a blanket and tuck it over Leighton's legs, perhaps smooth the lock of black hair back from his brow. He wanted to kick him awake and shout at him to pull himself together. He wanted to kiss him.

He turned away abruptly. That was more than enough of that. He meant to leave the library at once, but the gold lettering on the spine of a familiar volume caught his eye. It was *The Arabian Nights' Entertainment*, a book he'd read so many times as a boy that his copy of it had worn to shreds. Arthur had read it to him first.

Tom crossed silently to the shelf and pulled the book down, running his fingers over the familiar cover. It had soothed him through many a dreary day — why not see if it would have the same effect on William?

He tucked it under his arm and slipped from the library, shutting the door gently behind him and then taking the stairs two at a time to the second floor and William's bedchamber.

Carter answered Tom's soft knock. To Tom's surprise, he smiled and stepped back at once to let him inside. "Look who it is, sir," he said, turning his head to speak to William. "Mr. Drake's come to visit."

Tom had sat with William for a few minutes at a time, always with Leighton there, but he hadn't been to see William alone since that first morning. Now he understood how thoughtless he had been. William's face lit up at the sight of Tom, his thin cheeks creasing in a smile. Tom hid his horror at the tint of crimson that limned William's teeth.

"I hope I'm not disturbing you," he said.

"Not at all," William replied. "Carter, would you —" But his manservant was already bustling about, plumping William's pillows so that he could sit a little more upright and wrapping a woolen shawl about his bony shoulders. William turned to Tom and waved at the chair by the bed. "Sit down, and tell me how it is out of doors. I can tell you've been out."

Tom laughed a little unsteadily. "I apologize for my appearance. Stocking feet and damp hair aren't quite the thing when paying a call, I know."

"I can smell the rain on you," William said wistfully. "You brought in a breath of air with you. I'm grateful. Dr. Porter won't allow me to have a window open no matter how I beg, and Carter follows his every direction as if he spoke with Engar's own voice."

William stopped, his chest heaving up and down, and coughed horribly. Carter put a kerchief to his mouth. It came away stained with blood. Tom knew he ought to avert his eyes, ought to preserve what of William's dignity he could by pretending not to see. But he couldn't, and not just from morbid fascination. Flinching from William's illness would be almost more of a betrayal, and of a more fundamental kind.

William finally drew a full breath, though it rasped in his throat. "Forgive me. I know it's — not a pleasant thing to see."

Driven by some impulse he could neither understand nor control, Tom shifted forward in his chair and laid his hand over William's where it lay curled and clawlike on the coverlet. "Don't. Don't apologize for this. You deserve to feel comfortable at least, in your own bed. If it makes you less so to have me here, only say so, and I'll go."

"No. I'd rather have the company." William's hand moved just a little beneath his own, and Tom gave it a quick, awkward squeeze before he sat back again.

The silence that fell was more awkward still. Tom cleared his throat. "I brought this book from the library," he offered abruptly. "I don't know if you care for this sort of thing. But I loved it as a boy, read it to pieces. I thought I'd —" He couldn't finish, certain that he had already made a dreadful fool of himself. He'd thought he would, what, read to William? Like one would to a child laid up with a cold in the head? He gripped the book so hard he felt the spine bend. "I should go."

William's head dropped back against the pillow, and he sighed. "Please don't," he said softly, arresting Tom in the act of standing. Tom sank back down again. "I think you meant to read to me. I'd like that." He smiled faintly. "Perhaps it'll keep me here for a thousand and one more nights, you never know."

Tom had no reply to that, so he simply opened the book, drew a deep breath of the stuffy, medicinal air of the room, and began to read.

Tales of Arabian magic wouldn't keep William on this earth, of that he was quite certain. But Tom would, somehow. He would damn well make sure of it.

Chapter Nine

MAL STARED DOWN at the coffee cup in his hand, wishing it were brandy. Time enough for that when he returned downstairs; for now, he needed to make himself into something resembling a human if he meant to sit with Will a while.

He'd woken in perfect darkness, panicked, and flailed himself quite off the sofa and onto the floor, making a sufficient ruckus that the door had burst open to reveal a footman holding a single candle that illuminated his terrified face. It took Mal a moment to recognize the library, and a further moment to understand that the look of fear on the lad's face was because of him.

As disoriented as he was, he'd only managed to crawl to his feet, mutter a demand for coffee in his bedchamber at once, and stagger up the stairs. He'd hidden in his dressing room when a servant brought the coffee, too befuddled with sleep and grief and shame to even attempt to interact with another person. No doubt he'd need to raise everyone's wages. It hardly mattered.

A dull sound startled him out of his fugue. Mal listened a moment, hearing only the tapping of the rain against the windows. There it was again: a knock at his door. Mal frowned. Surely behaving like an ogre ought to come with the few perquisites of being thought a monster, such as being left the bloody hell alone?

"Come in," he growled. Well. At least he sounded the part. He cleared his throat and took a searing sip from his cup.

Tom stepped inside, coat and waistcoat abandoned somewhere and shirt open at the top to reveal a triangle of pale, smooth skin. The coffee went down the wrong way and Mal choked, spilled coffee across his knuckles, and dropped the cup to the table by the fireplace with a clatter and a curse. He wiped his stinging fingers on his shirt. He'd slept in it for the gods only knew how many hours, and he'd been sweating brandy the whole time. The damn thing would likely need to be burnt in any case. And of course, of *course*, he hadn't taken the time to change his linen before Tom walked in looking like all of the fantasies Mal tried to ignore in the middle of the night.

Tom calmly shut — and locked, Mal noted with some surprise — the door behind him and advanced into the room, stopping just out of arm's reach. There was something very wrong with Tom. He was here in Mal's bedchamber, for one thing, but it wasn't like him to miss such an opportunity for mockery as Mal had just afforded him. Mal's hackles rose. Something was very wrong.

"What do you want?"

Tom raised one eyebrow. "What I want isn't really the point. You'd do better to ask me why I'm here."

Mal gritted his teeth. *Damn* Tom. Damn him and his games, and damn his thrice-damned beautiful face and lean, seductive body. He hadn't the patience for this. Worse, he didn't have the self-control. Mal needed to fight or he needed to fuck, something to relieve the pressure building in his brain, mounting until he thought he might blow to pieces from the force of it.

"You have ten seconds to say. What. You. Mean. Or get the hell out." Mal grated the words out through jaws that felt as tightly clamped as an iron vise.

Tom just looked at him levelly, unintimidated. Resigned? Mal felt another prickle of unease. "Very well. I'm here to consummate our marriage."

Mal's blood surged, racing through every vein like fire and setting him alight from within. "What did you say?" he asked hoarsely.

"You heard me perfectly well." Tom sounded cold, but far from cool and composed. "William's condition hasn't improved. Unless Dr. Porter had something optimistic to report today?"

That faint note of hope pulled Mal's brimming temper to the surface. "And what the fuck do you care either way?" he snarled, stepping right up to Tom so closely that their chests brushed. Bright, searing desire flared in him, battling his resentment. "Your damned blessing was supposed to have helped. And all you've done is mope about the house and —"

"*I've* been moping about the house?" Tom demanded, cheeks flaring red and eyes bright with fury. He shoved Mal's chest, making him stumble back a step. "You're the one who's drunk a cellar's worth of brandy. *You're* the one who came up with this hare-brained plan to use my blessing to save William's life, and how *dare* you act as if you're the one who deserves sympathy? Or pity? William's dying, and I'm the one trying to think of a way to stop it!"

"You? You're bored and restless and looking for a

fuck, and you're telling me I'm ..." Mal stuttered to a halt. His immediate impulse was to fight back, to defend himself against Tom's accusations of drunkenness and self-pity — but Tom was right. He shook his head to clear it; mostly he succeeded in making it spin a bit, but the pause allowed him to review Tom's words and really consider his meaning. "A way to stop it," he said slowly. "A way — you think the blessing hasn't taken effect because our marriage is only in name."

Tom glared at him and raised a scornful eyebrow. "I'm glad you could catch up," he said, contempt dripping from every word. "Yes. That's what I think. Did you really believe I'd come to you because — because I *wanted* you?"

For a heart-stopping moment, that was indeed what Mal had thought. "I never know why you do anything," he said, with an honesty that took him by surprise.

It seemed to have the same effect on Tom; his other eyebrow shot up to join its fellow. "A man must have his secrets." Tom's effortlessly seductive tenor made the words far more salacious than Tom had probably intended. Or perhaps not. One corner of Tom's lips curved up in a little half-smile that went right to Mal's cock. Perhaps he knew quite well what he was about. Thank the gods he was unaware of just how little seduction Mal would require. "My motives in this case are quite simple, though. We married for a purpose, and we haven't seen it through. We ought to try."

Mal narrowed his eyes. Simple motives? Tom? Particularly since kindness was the only simple motive available, and that couldn't possibly be right.

"Why do you care? And why now, why tonight? You

told me to stay away from you."

Tom crossed his arms and shifted his feet, his eyes darting from the fire to the coffee cup — anywhere but Mal. "I spent part of the morning with William," he admitted.

Mal's gut clenched. "You promised you wouldn't tell him —"

"And I didn't!" Tom snapped. "I didn't tell him anything, though I felt a right bloody bastard sitting there and listening as he told me —" Tom's voice broke. The movement of his elegant throat as he swallowed was nearly mesmerizing. "He told me how glad he was that you'd have me to comfort you when he was gone."

"Oh," was all Mal could say. He turned blindly toward the fireplace, crossing to lean his forehead against the mantel. He thumped his head on it gently, squeezing his eyes shut against the prickling sensation of tears. Mal had thought he had no more left.

"I'm not doing this for you."

Mal couldn't turn to face him. Not until he had himself more in control. "I thought you were doing it for my fortune."

A long silence followed, underlined by the constant tattoo of the rain. "I was at first," Tom said, very quietly. "Now —" He laughed, a miserable little sound that struck Mal like a stone flung from a catapult at his crumbling defenses. "Now I'm doing it for him." Gods, but Mal couldn't bear it. To have Tom care for Will, to show himself ready to sacrifice for his sake, cast Tom in a light Mal couldn't afford to see him in. Not if he wished to remain as distant from his husband as he had to for his own well-being.

He could not possibly like Tom. It would be a disaster.

But the searing jealousy that caught him by the throat was a greater disaster still. Tom wouldn't lift a finger for Mal's sake, much less spread his legs. But for Will — it seemed he would do anything necessary for Will. And why not? Even sick and wasted and dying, Will had ten times Mal's charm, decency, humor, and wit. Anyone would love him. And if Will recovered, once Mal had gotten the merest taste of how sweet Tom could be, there would be nothing standing in the way of Tom and Will finding real happiness together. Certainly not Mal. He might lose his dearest friend and the man he — never mind that, and *Tom*, all at one stroke, but he'd step aside. His pride would demand it, if nothing else.

Mal steeled himself, breathed in deeply, and turned. Tom stood with his chin tilted up and his hands twisting together — half defiant, and half nervous, and altogether too appealing for words.

"You're right," Mal said, with admirable steadiness, he felt. "It's worth the attempt."

Tom laughed bitterly. "Yes. I rather thought you might be willing to make the sacrifice. Generous of you."

"What are you implying? That I don't want to fuck you, or that I do? Either way, I'm not sure why it would anger you." Which one angered Tom the more suddenly seemed like a crucial piece of information, and Mal held his breath, hoping he'd be goaded into answering.

No such luck. "It hardly matters, as long as you can get it up."

"I'm certain I can manage," Mal said, with

breathtaking understatement.

Tom shrugged. "Then that's all we need. Besides this, of course." He pulled a small bottle from the pocket of his breeches and tossed it onto the bed. Tom drew his shirt over his head in one smooth motion and dropped it carelessly to the floor. His hands went immediately to the placket of his breeches, and Mal stood all but paralyzed, only his hands twitching with the desperate need to touch Tom everywhere at once.

Mal didn't know if he'd ever seen anything more perfect, from the breadth of Tom's smooth white shoulders to the narrow taper of his waist, from the scattering of soft hair on his chest to the fine line that led down to where his hands were busy with his buttons. Tom turned to give Mal his profile. The muscular roundness of his arse was just enough to fit in both of Mal's hands.

"Gods, Tom," he whispered. He moved, drawn to Tom like iron to a lodestone. Mal stretched out a hand and laid it gently, almost reverently, on the small of Tom's back just above that tantalizing, delectable curve.

Tom jerked away. "No," he said flatly, and slid the last button free.

Mal's hand clenched on empty air. "What the hell do you mean, *no*?" Did Tom expect to fuck without touching?

The breeches slid to the floor, and Tom tugged the laces on his drawers and pushed them down to follow. Tom stood quite nude, candlelight gleaming on his skin like flecks of gold in alabaster. His cock hung almost limp against his thigh.

"I mean *no*, Leighton. There's no need to make this anything other than what it is. This is — a formality. Like signing the temple marriage register." Tom looked up to meet Mal's eyes, his own wide and dark.

"The hell it is." Mal shifted just a little, until he could feel the warmth of Tom's body. He could smell him, too, just the faintest fragrance of lavender and spice, a scent that drove Mal nearly to distraction. If he bent his head just a fraction he could bury his face in Tom's mass of waving hair, open his mouth and taste him, in that hollow just behind his ear. Breathe him in. "This isn't a bloody formality."

"It is," Tom said, almost desperately, as if trying to convince himself as much as Mal. "I'll prepare myself and put my arse up and all you need to do —"

A near-feral growl erupted from Mal's chest, a sound he hadn't known he could make. "I'll *prepare* you. And you'll put your arse wherever I damn well want it."

Tom let out a ragged breath and his eyes dilated until their bright blue was nearly lost in a sea of gleaming black. "This isn't for pleasure. It's not for us. I mean, it's not for you. It's not for me in any case," he panted. "I don't want this."

"No?" Mal looked down pointedly at Tom's cock, which had come to half-mast, the head flushed to a ruddy deep pink. Mal's mouth watered at the sight. He glanced up to find Tom had followed his gaze, his cheeks turning as rosy as his lovely prick. Tom bit his lower lip and Mal nearly groaned aloud.

"No," Tom whispered.

"Sit down," Mal said, his tone leaving no room for argument.

Tom's arse hit the edge of the bed like he'd been taken

out at the knees. His breath came in harsh bursts, and he fisted his hands in the coverlet to either side of his thighs. Tom's cock stood out between them, fully hard, long and lovely. Whatever he might wish he wanted, his body responded to Mal's — *he* responded, and Mal's heart sang with triumph. He would make Tom beg before the night was over — beg to be touched, beg to be fucked, beg for *Mal*.

Slowly, savoring his own anticipation nearly as much as the way Tom's knuckles went white around the bedding, Mal went to his knees. Tom's feet were still caught in his clothing; that would need to be dealt with first. He wrapped a hand around one of Tom's ankles, lifting his foot free of his drawers and breeches. Mal repeated the process on the other side, shoved the clothing out of the way, and gently pushed Tom's legs apart. He let his hands linger on Tom's thighs, thumbs stroking the tender backs of his knees.

Mal could feel the faintest vibration beneath his hands: Tom was trembling. He hid his exultant smile by leaning in and taking the head of Tom's cock between his lips. He'd meant to undo Tom, but the first taste of him left Mal the one with his head swimming and his cock so hard it hurt, trapped at just the wrong angle by his tight trousers.

He kept his hands where they were, using only his mouth to hold Tom steady while he plied his tongue in every way he knew how. Circles, and little flicks, and then at last he went all the way down, drawing Tom's cockhead into his throat.

Tom moaned, and his hips bucked up. Mal slid his hands up to the tops of Tom's thighs and held him down hard, keeping the slow pace he'd set. This had been meant only as a way to bring Tom to heel, but he wanted — he *needed* more of the sweet-salt of Tom's skin, the throbbing heat of him on Mal's tongue, as he'd never needed anything.

He drew back to take a breath, and Tom was suddenly in motion, both of his hands tangled in Mal's hair. "Please," he gasped. Mal stopped, just the very tip of Tom's cock caught between his lips. "Please don't —" Tom swallowed hard. Wild-eyed and flushed, he made an image Mal wished he could engrave forever in his mind. Every drop of blood seemed to freeze in his veins as he waited for Tom's next words; another refusal, when Mal had already done everything in his power to seduce him, would be final. At last Tom said, his voice a hoarse whisper, "Please don't stop."

Chapter Ten

"PLEASE DON'T STOP." The words slipped out, Tom hardly recognizing his own voice. Leighton's hair slid between his fingers like strands of raw silk.

And Leighton's eyes — pools of inky black, glittering with a harsh desire that Tom knew would be his undoing if he couldn't find the courage to end this before it was too late. The hands on Tom's thighs tightened, their grip almost painful, and heat shot through him, lighting every nerve with longing.

It was already too late. He needed more of that touch, more of Leighton's hands tearing the pleasure from him, more of Leighton's mouth, goddess, his mouth, hotter and more skilled than any Tom had ever felt. Or perhaps it was just that it was Leighton — proud, controlled, overbearing Leighton, on his knees with Tom's aching prick between his lips.

Leighton smiled around it, somehow keeping it in his mouth all the while. It was the smile of a hawk with a mouse in its talons — a mouse that had just begged to be devoured. Suddenly shifting his grip, Leighton shoved Tom's legs up so that his feet left the floor and landed on the edge of the bed, spreading him impossibly, obscenely open. The bed creaked in protest as Tom toppled onto his back, his hands still buried in Leighton's thick hair. He pushed Leighton's head down and Leighton allowed it, sucking his cock down, and down, until Tom felt the head press into his throat. His balls drew up as Leighton bobbed up and down, and he was just there, on the brink —

Cold air hit his wet cock as Leighton pulled off. Tom cried out and tried to pull Leighton back down, but he jerked his head away. "Bloody hell, you fucker, I'm so close, I'm —" A low laugh, and then Tom cut off with a wail as Leighton wrapped one big hand around his cock, ducked his head, and pressed his tongue against Tom's hole.

His tongue pushed *in*. Tom had been fucked before, but quickly, furtively, always in the dark to keep Mirreith's mark hidden — and to maintain control of his responses, to keep the upper hand even when he was the one bent over. He couldn't have kept control then if his life depended on it. Tom's back arched, and his moan echoed off the ceiling as he spent, and spent, and spent, until he was limp and sweat-soaked and panting.

Slowly, Leighton released his oversensitive cock, letting it come to rest gently against Tom's stomach. Tom kept his eyes closed. Looking down at Leighton, framed as he would be by Tom's splayed legs and come-spattered body, was quite impossible.

Leighton shifted slightly and pressed an open-mouthed kiss to the very top of his thigh — to Mirreith's twisted sigil, the mark Tom had hidden his whole life, had hated, had wished with every bit of his soul he could cut from his own flesh like a cancer.

Something like a sob tore out of Tom's chest, and he

turned his head as far as he could into the bedclothes. He had expected Leighton to be rough and careless in his victory, to turn him over and thrust inside at once. Tom wouldn't have tried to stop him.

Warm hands wrapped around Tom's ankles and lowered his feet gently back to the floor. More kisses followed, up one leg to his hip — a nibble there, just the faintest scrape of Leighton's teeth, enough to make Tom give a quick, convulsive shiver — and then over his belly to his chest. Leighton lingered on his throat, his breath feverishly hot.

"Tom," Leighton murmured, the word a caress against the curve of his jaw. When Tom didn't answer, Leighton took his chin in one hand. "Tom. Look at me."

That note of command was impossible to resist. Tom yielded, turned his head, and opened his eyes. Leighton's gaze met his steadily, and he nodded as if in approval.

Leighton stroked his thumb over Tom's cheek. "I'm going to fuck you now. Do you have any further objections?"

A shake of the head was all Tom could manage. The same heavy helplessness he'd felt the night they married had descended upon him again — a feeling of complete inevitability, as if Leighton had cast a geas upon him and he could do nothing but blindly obey.

The hand on Tom's face gripped a little more tightly. "I want you to say it, Tom. Tell me what you want." That voice, low and gravelly. Tom felt its pull somewhere deep within, and he couldn't begin to resist.

"I want you to fuck me, Leighton," he said slowly, his tongue feeling thick and unfamiliar as he formed the words. The sting of humiliation warred uncomfortably with the warmth that spread through him as he spoke, something like arousal — and a bit of that sparked in his belly, too — but more like satisfaction, the sense of having done what he ought.

Leighton frowned. "Try again." Tom stared at him uncomprehendingly. What more could Leighton want from him? He'd done precisely as he was told. Leighton sighed, and Tom caught a hint of brandy and his own release on Leighton's hot breath. His cock filled a little more, recovering far more quickly than he would have thought possible. "My name, Tom. Try again."

Swallowing did nothing for the lump in Tom's throat. "Malcolm," he whispered hoarsely. That still sounded wrong — too formal, not what he would want. "Mal."

Leighton's eyes widened and his whole body went tense. "That's right." He leaned down and brushed his lips over Tom's, coaxing rather than demanding. "Say it again, properly this time."

Tom arched up, straining to reach Leighton's mouth, but he pulled back, his hand sliding from Tom's jaw to his throat and pinning him with his grip.

"Not yet." Leighton dug his fingers in a little harder. That pressure sent shockwaves through Tom's body, every limb tingling and his cock hardening almost to the point of pain. Tom cried out, a sharp, desperate sound. "Tom," Leighton said, sounding desperate himself.

"Mal," Tom choked out. "Mal, for the gods' sakes, *fuck me.*"

And then those lips were on his, muffling Mal's groan. His tongue swept in and Tom met it with his own, tangling and frantic. The full weight of Mal's body pressed down on him and he rutted up, rubbing his cock against the fabric of Mal's trousers and spreading his legs to bring him somehow impossibly closer.

Tom tried to fit his hands between them and get at Mal's buttons, but there wasn't room. He tore his mouth away, his lips bruised and stinging. "Off," he gasped.

Mal muttered something that sounded like agreement and sat back, his knees braced against Tom's inner thighs. The shirt went first, torn over Mal's head and flung to the side. Tom's mouth went dry. For all his deceptive leanness when in his well-tailored clothing, Mal had the broad chest and perfectly formed muscles of a man accustomed to using his body actively and often. Whorls of black hair framed flat brown nipples that Tom longed to trace with his tongue, lick and kiss before moving down and exploring the ridges of Mal's abdomen.

He pushed himself up, legs protesting the strained angle, and pressed his face to Mal's chest, opening his mouth to taste his skin. Mal made a strangled sound that Tom felt vibrating against his lips.

Big hands cradled the back of his head, pinning him in place. Tom kissed Mal's sternum, salt and heat on his tongue. He wrapped his arms around Mal's back and kneaded the muscles there. It wasn't enough, he needed, he *needed* — and he clenched his legs around Mal, held onto his sides, and twisted, bringing all his strength to bear.

Mal let out a surprised *oof* as he landed on his back with Tom straddling his hips. Tom spent a split second enjoying Mal's startlement, eyes wide and lips parted, before he bent down and put his mouth to the skin just above his trousers. He drew the flesh into his mouth and sucked, hard, making Mal's abdomen tense and flex, earning himself a deep moan of shocked desire.

The last time they'd almost fucked, Mal had torn Tom's last decent suit of clothing. Tom seized the placket of Mal's trousers and jerked it open with a resounding rip, the buttons left hanging by threads.

He looked up and met dark, hooded eyes. "Turnabout is fair play?" Mal asked. "You won't get away with it for long." Tom shivered, hoping he meant it.

Tom slid his hand into the opening of Mal's drawers and drew out his prick, never breaking away from that hot gaze. He learned its shape and heft by touch, stroking up and down, feeling the weight of it. It had to be too large to fit inside him, thick and heavy, and Tom wanted nothing more than to prove his own fears wrong. Mal's hands landed on Tom's hips. His fingers dug in deeply enough to bruise, as if he could barely keep himself in check. Still, he let Tom do as he would, only letting out one short, broken sound when Tom swiped his thumb over the swollen head of his cock.

Finding the bottle of oil he'd brought required looking away, and as he did, he ventured one glance down at the cock in his hand. It looked even larger than it felt, only half of it fitting in Tom's hand. The bottle nearly slipped out of Tom's grasp, but he managed to press it against one of Mal's hands.

Tom had thought he'd seen Mal lose his composure and give in to his desires before. He was wrong. In an instant he was crushed against Mal's chest, one arm like an iron band around his back and Mal's mouth on his, hungry and all-consuming. He had never been kissed like this, devoured like this, with Mal's tongue fucking his mouth and teeth nipping at his lips. Tom writhed, rubbing frantically against him until their cocks met and pressed together in the most delicious friction he had ever felt.

Slick fingers probed between the cheeks of his arse, giving him a moment's warning before two were suddenly inside him, the stretch and burn of it too much all at once. Tom's whole body jerked, but Mal had him pinned like a butterfly, caught between that kiss and his fingers, thrusting in and out and curling to find the spot inside Tom that lit his every nerve with wildfire.

Mal pulled his fingers out again and Tom cried out, tearing his mouth away from Mal's and burying his face in his neck.

"Come on," Mal said, low and frantic, and tugged his hip, shifting him up Mal's body. He felt Mal's hand busy between his legs slicking his own cock, and then the head was right there, demanding entrance, hot and thick.

It would hurt. Tom knew it would hurt, but he'd never wanted anything more than the pain of it. He flexed down, hard, just as Mal wrapped his hands around Tom's hips again and pushed.

Mal's cock thrust inside him in one motion, all the way to the hilt.

For a moment everything stopped, and Tom hung suspended in time with all sensation numbed away. And then it all rushed in again, the fullness and the burn and the way he thought he might split in two, Mal's prick filling him so completely he couldn't draw breath.

Mal held him by the hips, moved his own, and thrust. Again, and again, so deeply that Tom's teeth rattled. Tom keened, clutched Mal's shoulders, and took it, bracing himself against Mal's chest and opening himself fully.

Words washed over him: *beautiful* and *Tom* and *sweetheart* and *tight* and *perfect*, words he never would have thought to hear in Mal's deep voice, not for him. Mal's cock moved over and over that nub of pleasure inside him, and his own slid against Mal's body. He shook in every limb, dug his fingers into Mal's shoulders, and spiraled into a climax that ripped him apart.

Mal shouted, and tensed, and spilled into Tom in burst after burst of heat.

The last of Tom's energy faded into nothing, and he let his head rest on Mal's shoulder. Mal's heart thumped wildly beneath his cheek. He was sticky, and still spread open lewdly across Mal's body, and still stuffed full of his prick. Tom sighed, closed his eyes, and let himself fall.

Chapter Eleven

*G*ODS, SWEETHEART, *you're so perfect, so beautiful, Tom...* His own words echoed in Mal's ears. It would have been so much better if he could have pretended he hadn't meant them, that they had been the ravings of a man lost in the temporary madness of climax.

Mal had meant every syllable. Tom's weight lay heavy on his torso, making breathing a challenge — Tom was smaller than Mal, but hardly delicate. Warm breath wafted against the side of Mal's neck, a little too hot and humid in Mal's current state of sweaty lassitude. The stickiness of Tom's release between their stomachs and the slow withdrawal of Mal's softening cock were hardly pleasurable sensations. Tom's hair was tickling Mal's ear and chin, and Mal's legs were going to grow stiff if he didn't rise.

It was utterly, completely perfect. Mal's hands still rested on Tom's hips, their curves just the right fit. Tom seemed to have fallen asleep — or Mal had just fucked him senseless, a thought that gave him a surge of chest-expanding satisfaction — so he felt he could get away with stroking one hand up Tom's back, caressing as much of his lover's smooth skin as he could reach. His hand came to rest on the nape of Tom's neck, and he idly played with his hair, letting the satiny strands sift through his fingers.

Perhaps if his emotions were less raw he might have been able to hold back something of himself. But after weeks, months, of watching Will slowly die, he had few defenses left, and Tom had effortlessly destroyed those last remnants of Mal's resistance.

Mal had only just spent himself inside Tom's sweet body and already he wanted to take him again. Slowly this time, with Tom on his back, his arms around Mal's waist. Smiling. The thought of kissing Tom's smiling lips, nipping his throat and making him laugh, seeing joy light up his clear blue eyes — Mal was quite completely and utterly fucked, and he squeezed his eyes shut in a futile effort to banish the fantasy.

They had consummated their marriage. There was no more reason for him to touch Tom, and the moment he woke and pulled away, that would be all Mal would ever have.

Mal buried his face in Tom's hair, greedily taking in that light, sweet, spicy scent that seemed to breathe from Tom's skin. Part of his blessing, perhaps — only someone touched by the divine could smell so lovely, feel so lovely, could enchant every one of Mal's senses and wash away his capacity for rational thought.

Tom stirred, and Mal froze, hoping he would go back to sleep and allow Mal just a few more minutes of holding him in his arms. And then he felt the moment Tom realized where he was, and upon whom he'd been sleeping so peacefully.

"Oh," Tom said, sounding anything but peaceful. He jolted upright, dislodging Mal's cock, winced, and stared wildly down at Mal as if he were waking into a nightmare.

"Oh bloody buggering *goddess*."

Tom shoved himself away, scrambling off of Mal with none of his usual grace. He staggered as his feet hit the floor and righted himself by catching at the armchair set by the table. Tom crossed his arms over the back and slumped there, breathing heavily, his head hanging down. Candlelight gleamed on the wetness trickling down Tom's thighs.

The sharp, lancing pain in Mal's breast left him struggling for breath. A kiss. He would have killed a man to have a kiss when Tom woke. He pushed up on his elbows. "Don't think it was Mirreith who buggered you," he drawled. "Although that would be something to see."

"Sod off," Tom said, muffled by his arms. By more than his arms?

But no. Mal couldn't let himself hope for a moment that Tom felt anything of what he did. Tom cared for Will, and he was stubborn enough to insist upon trying to accomplish what they'd set out to do with this foolish marriage. But that was all. An abandoned fiancé, a former wife who despised him enough to divorce him while still abed from childbirth, and above all, the look on Tom's face when he'd asked Mal how much he'd pay for his arse — Mal reminded himself of all of it, forced himself to remember. Any softness in Tom wasn't for him, if it existed at all.

Mal rolled to his side and reached for the bell rope, giving it a vicious tug. "I'm going to have a bath. So if you don't want to be standing there with my spend all over you when they answer the bell, you might want to sod off yourself."

Tom turned his head to glare, and Mal nearly lost what little was left of his mind at the sight of Tom bent over and peeking at Mal over his shoulder. He spun to the washstand and poured himself a glass of water. "If I wasn't clear enough, get out."

Quick footsteps and the rustling of clothing told him Tom was moving to do just that, and Mal clenched his hand around the glass. The rain had stopped at last, and Mal could hear Tom's breaths, fast and angry.

A cry from down the hall startled Mal badly enough that the glass fell from his hand and cracked against the washstand, spilling water down his legs.

"Mr. Leighton!" That was Carter's voice, high and panicked. "Mr. Leighton, please come quickly!"

His trousers, where the bloody hell were his — and then they appeared right in front of his face, dangling from Tom's hand.

Mal shoved his legs into them and dashed away. One button would need to do. Will's door stood open at the end of the corridor, and the sounds coming from the bedchamber made the hair rise on the back of Mal's neck. Sweat broke out all over him and panic bubbled up with the bile in his throat. He ran, following Carter's cries for help.

The sight that met him as he skidded to a stop in Will's doorway near felled him. Will sprawled across his bed, nightshirt rucked up and torn, his eyes open but rolling back in his head until only the whites were visible. He wasn't moving, not so much as the twitch of an eyelash.

Mal caught his weight on the doorframe with a shaking hand. "Carter," he breathed, a near-inaudible rasp.

"Is he —"

"No, sir," Carter gasped. The lad looked as if he'd gone three rounds with a professional boxer. His neckcloth hung down around his collar, which had been pulled askew, he was soaking wet, and on top of it his left eye was swollen almost shut. Blood dripped from his lower lip. "He's alive. I've just felt his pulse. He had — he had some kind of fit. All his limbs went every which way, and I tried to hold him, but even as weak as he is..." Carter trailed off into a sob and roughly rubbed his sleeve over his eyes.

Now that Mal could breathe again, he noticed the broken crockery at Carter's feet. That explained the wet clothing, at least. "A lad I knew as a boy was epileptic. When he had a fit, he had the strength of a full-grown man. You couldn't have done more."

Carter nodded at that, because there was simply nothing else to be said. They both knew it. And after sending for Dr. Porter, cleaning Will up as best they could, and changing the bed linens, there came the worst part of all: sitting an anxious, useless vigil.

All the while, Mal could think of nothing but his own failings. While his cousin seized and frothed at the mouth, Mal had been lost in Tom, unaware of anything but his moans and the tight grip of his body. Any thought of consummating their marriage for Will's benefit had been on Tom's part; Mal had long since given up the pretense of wanting Tom for any reason besides his own helpless infatuation. He lied to Tom, and he lied to Will, but he had made a point of never lying to himself.

And now, waiting for Dr. Porter to come and render his verdict on Will's chances, Mal forced himself to face the truth: he would lose Will, and Tom had never been his to lose.

It had been nearly an hour since Mal ran to William's bedchamber, time that Tom had spent pacing his own, back and forth across the carpet, counting the blue roses in the pattern and then beginning again when he lost his place. Walking hurt, every step a reminder of how hard Mal had used him — or rather how hard he had used himself, riding Mal's cock like a wanton slut.

Tom strode across the room more quickly, cheeks heating, but it was no way to escape the memory of it.

In any case, sitting hurt more.

Goddess, but he wished he knew what was happening down the corridor. Nausea rose up at the thought of William lying dead, moments after he and Mal had…with a muffled moan, he spun on his heel again and all but ran across the room, ending up leaning against the wall with his head buried in his hands.

If William died, Tom would grieve, he knew that. And Mal's grief didn't bear thinking of. But if he'd just given himself — goddess, more than given himself, he'd *begged* for Mal's touch — for nothing, bared his most carefully hidden longings to a man who despised him, without even accomplishing the goal of William's recovery? It would be too much: failure, humiliation, the knowledge of his own worthlessness, grief and shame, all at once.

The hall clock began to chime; Tom held quite still and listened until he heard it sound eleven times. Almost two hours, now, since Carter called out in such terror. A moment later the crunch of gravel announced a carriage pulling up to the house, and Tom eased his door open and ran as lightly as possible to the top of the stairs. The butler himself went to open the front door, and Dr. Porter stepped inside.

Dizzy with relief, Tom tiptoed back to his own room. If the doctor had come at this time of night, William was alive.

For the first time since early childhood, Tom knelt by his bed and prayed to Mirreith, head bowed, tears he couldn't repress trickling down his cheeks and wetting the collar of his shirt. Thus far his blessing had earned him the hatred of his own father, a lifetime of secrecy, estrangement from his family, and a false marriage to the one man he might have truly chosen, given the opportunity. It had not inclined him toward religion.

Tonight, he needed someone in whom to confide, even a goddess he suspected hated him nearly as much as he resented her. Tom buried his face in the bedclothes and forced himself to breathe. He'd pushed the knowledge of his feelings far, far down, refusing to admit it to himself, but it seemed Mirreith would have the truth from him.

If they had met again under any other circumstances, and Mal had wanted him, truly wanted *him*, and not just his blessing and his body, Tom would have been his. Without question and without hesitation.

If consummating the marriage had no effect on William's health, then — but that didn't bear thinking of. Tom had sacrificed more than just his nonexistent virtue on the altar of William's well-being. He had lost his self-respect, his pride, and any possibility of hiding his heart from a husband who neither loved nor liked him.

Mal could have no doubts whatsoever about Tom's feelings. Tom's resistance had been a token effort. He was so tired of always fighting to conceal what he was. Honesty had been impossible with any of his former lovers, his fiancé, or his wife. He could never be open, never make love in the daylight, never forget how his family would despise him if they only knew. Tom choreographed every encounter.

Until Mal. Mal, who took charge of him so effortlessly Tom could do nothing but yield; Mal, who allowed Tom to feel, rather than think.

If Mirreith heard him, she gave no answer. Tom laid in bed for some time, listening for Dr. Porter or Mal in the corridor. At long last the silence gave way to the pattering of rain and the distant boom of thunder, and Tom slipped into exhausted sleep.

Chapter Twelve

MAL WOKE TO A SENSE of utter disorientation and a sharp ache in his lower back. Blinking the crust from his eyelids, he lifted his head and found himself gazing blearily at Will, who was sound asleep in his bed. Mal sat up and cursed the crick in his neck. The last thing he remembered was sitting by Will's bedside, straining to hear his cousin's shallow breaths over the crackling of the fire and the patter of the rain. He didn't remember slumping forward onto the edge of the bed; he must have passed out from sheer exhaustion.

It had taken nearly two hours for Dr. Porter to arrive, the servant sent for him having finally tracked him down at a cottage two miles outside the village. There was nothing he could do, he told Mal with the type of frowning, low-voiced sympathy that never boded well. Will would live, or he would not, but the fit had taken much of his strength. It was in the hands of the gods.

Mal had broken out into bitter laughter at that. It was perhaps lucky that Dr. Porter was accustomed to the odd reactions of his patients' relations.

Carter had given Mal one of Will's dressing gowns to wear over the trousers he'd pulled on half-buttoned when he fled his bedchamber, but his bare feet were chilled to numbness despite the thick rug they'd rested on overnight.

Mal stood slowly, cautiously stretching his back and feeling all the pains of a night spent in a chair in addition to sweeter aches in muscles well-used in the pursuit of pleasure.

Pleasure. What a woefully inadequate word for the sensations that overtook him in Tom's arms, buried in Tom's body. *He told me how glad he was that you'd have me to comfort you when he was gone.* Mal could almost find it funny. If Tom had truly been his husband, in the sense of a helpmate and friend and lover, it might have been enough to soften the blow of Will's loss. Tom could be thoughtful, he could be gentle; he'd proven it in the hours he spent reading to Will, conversing with him when he had the strength and simply sitting beside him and giving him the comfort of his presence when he didn't.

Mal wished he could resent it, could wonder why Tom offered such a generous ration of kindness to Will when he could spare not a whit of it for Mal. But he knew damn well why. It was Mal's own doing. He'd never given Tom the chance to be anything but the callous rake the world believed him to be, sneering at and berating him, seducing and mocking him. Who could possibly wish to reveal more of his inner self to someone who'd behaved as Mal had — who could trust him?

He had no one to blame but himself. Self-knowledge was one of Mal's strengths; he had always prided himself on understanding his own mind and avoiding the self-delusions that other, weaker men fell into. It brought him a cold, self-righteous satisfaction, feeling himself above those who lied to themselves to preserve their own contentment.

The knowledge that he himself had destroyed his own

chances of any kind of happiness through his own cruelty brought him anything but satisfaction now. For the first time, he wondered if it might be better to be weak than to be confronted with the certainty of having hurt and alienated the one man whose love he might have wanted to win.

Mal didn't care if the rumors about Tom were all true, although he had begun to entertain some doubts. Even if the truth was worse than the gossip, it didn't matter. Tom had shown himself capable of putting his own needs aside for the benefit of someone else and of compassion where it counted most. He would help Mal see Will through his last days on earth, he knew that much. It would be a blessing to have that help, to have another person here to look after Will when Mal grew too overwhelmed by grief to remain calm in Will's presence, a blessing that would have nothing to do with Mirreith's supposed interest in Tom and everything to do with Tom himself.

It would have to do. And after that, Mal would let Tom go.

The fire had burned down to almost nothing in the hours Mal had slept. He'd sent Carter away when the doctor departed, as much to be alone with his own miserable thoughts as to give the lad a much-needed rest.

Mal added a few sticks and stirred the embers as silently as he could, but his stiff limbs made him clumsy, and the poker clattered against the hearth.

"Carter?" Will sounded no weaker than he had the day before, and Mal's heart lifted just a trifle. He stood and set the poker down.

"It's me, Will," he said, and crossed back to the bed.

Will blinked up at him, his jade-green eyes clearer than Mal had seen them in weeks. "Let me ring for Carter, and we'll see to you."

Will smiled. "Don't. Let the boy sleep. I don't need him when you're here to wait on me hand and foot."

Mal found himself smiling in response. "He's a deal more useful than I am."

"True enough." Will paused, frowned, and then said wonderingly, "Mal, I'm hungry."

It took a moment for that to sink into Mal's sleep-addled brain. "Truly?" It had taken his and Carter's combined efforts to persuade Will to swallow eleven spoonfuls of gruel the day before. Mal had been counting how many bites of food Will managed to keep down for more than a month. He tugged the bell rope, violently enough that the bell downstairs probably all but jumped off the wall. "What do you want? Anything, if it's not in the kitchens I'll send out for it. I'll go myself. The season's wrong for fruit but I know of a hothouse —"

"Calm yourself," Will said, with a ghost of his old laugh. "You know I've never been particular. But those scones that Mrs. Dettridge makes, with the currants? If she happened to bake some of those?"

Mal outright grinned at that. "With butter. And clotted cream. And jam, of course." His own stomach gave an interested rumble, drawing another chuckle from Will, the sweetest sound Mal had ever heard. Will would live, and Mirreith had paid attention after all.

"No," Dr. Porter said, his lined face grave but his tone perhaps a little annoyed. Mal had sent for him again while the kitchen produced the requested scones, and it was likely he hadn't even had a glimpse of his own house between visits. He still had a splash of blood on his shirtfront from attending the birth, and his graying hair stood up in tufts. "We mustn't get ahead of ourselves. I absolutely cannot guarantee that Mr. Leighton will recover, and false hope can be —"

"False hope? *False hope?*" Mal turned and paced to the end of the library, spun again, and paced back. Dr. Porter stood calmly with his hands clasped behind his back. "He asked for breakfast! He hasn't been hungry in months. He's better! You must acknowledge that he's better." Mal turned the full force of his most commanding glare on the doctor, who stared back, entirely unmoved.

"I need not do anything of the kind," Dr. Porter said dryly. "Every illness is unique, as is every patient. No one would more pleased than I if Mr. Leighton were to experience a miraculous recovery. But in my," he cleared his throat and fixed Mal with a lowering glare of his own, "*extensive* experience, patients often rally briefly toward the end. This could be quite the opposite of the positive sign you want to see. In fact, the fit he had last night all but guarantees it."

The buzzing in Mal's ears reached a near-deafening pitch; he heard the doctor's voice, but everything after the word *end* blurred together . "He was hungry," Mal repeated helplessly, all the fight knocked out of him.

"I'll return tomorrow morning," Dr. Porter said, with just enough emphasis that Mal understood a summons before then would not be welcome, or possibly even heeded. More gently, he continued, "You should prepare yourself. Spend time with him. Enjoy this day to the fullest."

With that, he bowed and took his leave.

The empty library felt like a tomb after Dr. Porter's departure. Dust motes floated in the stray shaft of sunshine that had forced its way through the ever-present rainclouds, and the vacant chairs and looming bookcases felt as if they were squeezing in, compressing Mal's very soul.

He needed to get out. The doctor was right; he ought to savor every last moment he had with Will before it was too late. But he needed to move, to breathe, and inside the house it was impossible.

Mal stepped out the side door from the library onto the small terrace that ran the length of that wing of the house. Heavy clouds filled most of the sky, but the bit of sunlight that had penetrated the gloom of the library shone bright on the edge of the lake, creating a blindingly white glimmer amidst the gray. He set out to follow it, heedless of the cold. The thought of going back for his hat or overcoat made his flesh crawl. Mal broke into a run, racing toward the lake as if Death herself nipped at his heels.

The path around the lake led through a nearly natural wood as it curved away from the house, and Mal was deep in the shadow of the trees before he stopped, more winded than he ought to have been from such moderate exercise. So much time spent in a sickroom had left him out of condition.

Still, each breath felt like it went deeper into his lungs than any had in months. Each inhale burned, cold and raw, and his skin tingled where heated flesh met the damp chill of the air off the lake. The solitude soothed him, too. No one ever walked this way, except in the height of summer. It was too shaded, and there were no good spots for fishing on this side of the water.

Except that today someone had. As Mal rounded one of the path's many small turns, he caught a glimpse of something out of place: bottle-green, almost blending in with the woods, but too smooth and unnatural to be a part of them.

It was a coat: specifically, Tom's coat. Tom sat by the edge of the lake, propped against a mossy log with his legs stretched out in front of him and his booted ankles crossed. He had his head tipped back, gazing up at the sky, and his position put him in profile. Mal stilled, wanting to observe for a moment without being seen himself. He'd never been able to simply *look* at Tom like this, trace every contour of his face and memorize the lines of his long, lean body.

Mal had never taken any interest in art, but for the first time in his life he wished he could use a pen for more than scrawling a few letters to his relatives. To capture Tom as he was right then would have been a worthy use of such a talent.

"I could hear your footsteps, you know." Tom spoke without turning his head, and Mal gave a guilty start.

"How? The path's three inches deep in mud," Mal said without thinking.

Tom laughed, and Mal shivered. What would that sound feel like if Tom's face were pressed against his chest — no. "You have big feet."

Mal glanced down at his boots without thinking, blushed, and stomped his way through the underbrush, obnoxiously making as much noise as possible. It was childish, and petty, and the crunching of his boots was jarringly wrong in the peace of the morning. He felt it all the more when Tom didn't react, simply tipped his head back again and closed his eyes.

After a moment's hesitation, Mal lowered himself to the ground by Tom's side, wincing as the sopping-wet leaves beneath him instantly soaked his trousers through. But he'd sat close enough that his shoulder brushed Tom's, and the heat of that miniscule contact more than compensated, spreading through his every limb.

Though he wanted to turn and continue to stare at Tom, Mal looked out over the lake instead. "I'm sorry to disturb you." It came out sharply, and he clenched his fist against his thigh. Stupid, stupid, stupid, that he couldn't just for once apologize in a way that sounded as sincere as he meant it to be.

After a pause, Tom said, "You're not. It's your house, anyway."

Mal drew in a quick, pained breath, Tom's words reminding him of how much more than just Will he stood to lose. "It's not though. And if Will — Maberley will end up sold, I imagine."

Mal felt the slight shift in Tom's posture that meant he'd turned his head to look at him. "Sold? By whom?"

"Marcus. He's Will's heir."

"You're joking." Mal shook his head, unable to turn and meet Tom's eyes. He was in no state to hide his grief, his rage, at the thought of Will's home in the hands of strangers, sold off by a worthless cousin whose gambling debts mounted by the day. "You're not joking. Good goddess." Tom sounded as appalled by the idea as Mal felt. Gods, but he would have liked to kiss Tom right then.

"I suppose I could buy it from him, though I hate to see him get so much as a penny of mine." Mal had given that a great deal of thought, on long nights when he had little to occupy him but morbid imaginings. "I've always preferred it to my own house. It's a stuffy, confining old pile. Nothing like as beautiful as this. You'll hate it as much as I do, I make no doubt."

Mal didn't realize what he'd implied until Tom let out a soft sound, something between a gasp and a bitten-off curse. "It hardly matters what I'd think of it, since I'll never see it."

"Why not?" Mal turned at last, finding Tom's face close enough to his that he could have set his lips against Tom's with the slightest inclination of his head. "We're married. We'll need to go there eventually."

Tom licked his lips. Mal lost any thought of Maberley, or Will, or Marcus, and he bent that last inch and crushed Tom's soft mouth with his own.

Chapter Thirteen

Tom gripped Mal's shoulder and hauled him closer, returning the kiss with as much ferocity as it was given. Arousal flared to life within him, his cock stiffening so quickly the blood left his head in a rush. He moaned and tipped his head back as Mal moved down, nipping at his throat and sucking a mark into the delicate skin between his collarbones.

With a muffled oath, Mal ripped Tom's cravat from his neck and flung it away, baring more of his skin to Mal's hot mouth. Tom worked a hand between them and found Mal's prick, rubbing it through his clothing with a clumsy hand, the angle all wrong. It wrung a groan from Mal anyway, a sound that reverberated through Tom's chest and set his body singing, like a bell struck with just the right force. Mal thrust against his hand in desperate movements that showed how much he needed this.

But this wasn't enough. A quick fumble with their trousers half-undone would never be enough. Tom jerked away, pushing Mal back for leverage.

"I'm sorry," Mal gasped. "I didn't mean to —"

"If you say this was a mistake I might drag you to the lake and drown you."

Mal's eyes widened at that, and he reached out again; Tom dodged him and scrambled up on his knees, facing the log he'd been leaning on. He began to work his trouser buttons through the holes.

"What the devil are you doing?" Mal's hoarse voice sent shivers down his spine, like phantom fingernails scraping his skin.

Tom popped the last button out and shoved his trousers and drawers off his hips. He spread his legs as well as he could with the constriction of his clothing and leaned forward, bracing his forearms on the fallen trunk.

"I should think you might be able to work that out for yourself, Mal," he said, with acerbity born of near-stifling fear. He must look a sight, bent over and offering himself like this, kneeling in the muck of mud and leaves. Only a whore would want this. Mal would call him that, probably, and Tom almost welcomed it, so long as he fucked him too.

Mal's sharp inhale was loud in the silence of the woods, the sound of leaves and twigs stirring and crackling as he moved louder still. He slid his hand beneath the tails of Tom's coat, his cold fingers making Tom twitch.

"I won't hurt you." Tom could only laugh breathlessly; far too late for that. And then Mal added, "I can't take you like this without hurting you," and Tom understood.

"There's — in my coat pocket."

Mal's fingers dug in painfully. "Why would you have that out here?" His voice was as frigid as the lake, but there was an undercurrent in it that warmed Tom more than the sensation of Mal's body at his back. Jealousy was something, at least. Not care, precisely, but something.

"It's salve. My skin chaps in the cold. It'll serve the

purpose." Tom tried not to sound apologetic. It wasn't the manliest thing to admit to, and it was the kind of habit he'd been tormented for at school.

But Mal just leaned forward, pressing his chest to Tom's back and feeling about in his pocket with one hand while he slid the other around Tom's body, caressing beneath his shirt and stroking his fingers along the fine trail of hair that led down to Tom's cock. Tom felt Mal's hand close around the little jar just as Mal bit lightly at the nape of his neck. Tom stilled, the instinct of prey in the grasp of a predator. Mal bit again, harder, and Tom shuddered and let his head hang down between his arms.

"Don't move," Mal told him unnecessarily.

Slick fingers slid between the cheeks of Tom's arse. Tom sucked in a breath, trying to calm the racing of his heart, catching the scents of beeswax and chamomile mingling with the sharp odor of decaying leaves. Mal prepared him efficiently, without lingering or trying to tease. He pulled his fingers out too quickly, but Tom didn't protest. Mal wouldn't hurt him; Mal would take care of it, and of him. He closed his eyes and waited.

There was the wet sound of Mal stroking more of the salve onto his erection, and then Mal was inside him, pressing in deep and steady.

Mal didn't move for long, torturous seconds, letting Tom feel the length and girth of him filling his body. One of Mal's strong arms wrapped firmly around Tom's chest, while the other hand, the hand still slick with salve, took Tom's aching cock in a firm grip. A single stroke had Tom whimpering and forgetting he was supposed to be still, thrusting into Mal's hand as much as he could while bent and pinioned.

Mal understood it for the plea it was and shoved forward, hard and rough. He didn't hold back, pounding into Tom without mercy and without pause. Tom dug his fingers into the mossy bark beneath his hands, pieces of it tearing free and driving splinters into his palms. It went on and on, until sweat stuck Tom's shirt to his back and his knees went numb from being pressed into the ground.

He couldn't get enough friction to come, Mal's grip on his prick nearly punishing. "Mal, please," he groaned. "Please."

"You asked for it," Mal growled, and shifted his angle. His cock hammered into the precise spot inside Tom that sent sparks flying, igniting his climax from within. At the same time, he loosened his grip and slid his hand over Tom's cock, thumbing the head on the upstroke and massaging as he went down, again and again. The pressure built until the world spun around him, every part of him tingling almost to the point of pain. Mal thrust again, going impossibly deeper, and Tom let out an unearthly wail and painted the ground with his spend.

Mal fucked him through it, driving him against the fallen tree with vicious force and with only his arm around Tom's chest holding him up. At last he found his release, stilling and letting out a deep groan. He slumped down over Tom's back, his head resting between Tom's shoulderblades, his panting breaths ruffling the hair at the nape of Tom's neck.

A breeze ruffled through the woods, sending a few leaves skittering and chilling the sweat on Tom's brow. Mal was a blanket of heat along his back, though, and Tom laid his head on the backs of his hands and savored it.

All too soon, Mal pulled back with a sigh and carefully disengaged from Tom's aching body. Tom shivered.

"We need to get inside," Mal said. "You'll catch your death out here."

"You're the one without a coat," Tom managed. He clumsily boosted himself off the log and began to tug at his clothing, though his fingers were numb and shaking.

Mal took hold of the sides of his trousers. "Stand up, and I'll take care of the rest."

It was so much easier to simply do as Mal told him. Tom stood, Mal's hands warm and steadying against his thighs, and when Mal tugged his clothing up and reached around to do up the buttons, Tom leaned his head back against Mal's shoulder with a little contented sigh he couldn't suppress.

Mal's fingers lingered a moment when he was done. He nuzzled against the side of Tom's neck before he let go and stepped back, slowly, so Tom could catch his balance.

Tom looked about him for his cravat, finding it tangled on the ground with one end in a shallow pool of muddy water. He bent and picked it up, wincing a little at the movement. When he looked back at Mal, the man had an all-too-knowing glint in his eyes.

"Oh, shut it," Tom said.

Mal only grinned at him, and Tom blinked, his breath arrested for a moment. Goddess, but Mal was — not beautiful, though Tom felt the word might apply, but he was extraordinary, in his strength and masculine solidity, all broad shoulders and long legs and wind-blown black hair, his thick eyebrows and the slight twist to his lips only making him more imperfectly perfect.

Tom smiled helplessly back at him — and Mal looked away suddenly, his own smile fading to nothing.

"Think of an explanation for your appearance." Mal's tone was one of strict practicality. "Perhaps you took a tumble over a fallen branch."

That hurt more than it should have. "We are married. Practically newlyweds. Wouldn't it be expected —"

"No," Mal said shortly. And then, just as Tom felt he might crumple into the mud with humiliation, he added, "This was — just for us. It's not for servants to gossip about."

Pleasure suffused Tom like hot brandy. "At least if I tell them I took a tumble, it'll be the truth." He tossed Mal a saucy wink and had the satisfaction of seeing him flush. "But perhaps I can sneak up the back stairs. I must look a sight." He tried to brush some of the leaves from the knees of his trousers, only succeeding in coating his hands with streaks of mud.

"You do, at that." Tom glanced up. For just an instant, he caught Mal's eyes, and that heated gaze was everything he could ever want.

Mal looked away and set off for the path, and Tom followed, for once entirely without anything to say.

They took the path side by side, though Tom thought Mal was careful to keep a little distance. What would it be like to reach out, twine his fingers with Mal's, stroll this pleasant wood as lovers? He was too much a coward to risk Mal's certain rejection, and he stuffed his hands into his coat pockets.

At last the silence between them became suffocating,

too full of all the words Tom couldn't bring himself to speak. "I saw Carter this morning," he ventured, unable to bear it a moment longer. "He said William was better today." He swallowed, hardly daring to voice the hope that had been unfurling within him since his conversation with Carter a few hours before. "Do you think — could last night —"

"I thought so. But Dr. Porter seems to think it's not such a good turn."

"But if he's improved, how can that be for the worse?"

Mal grimaced. "I'm not a doctor," he said heavily. "But Dr. Porter says he's seen this before, that a patient can 'rally briefly before the end,' I think he put it. I don't know what to think," he finished, almost too low for Tom to make it out.

Perhaps it was Tom's urgent longing to have his marriage to Mal mean something, anything; perhaps it was that he needed, more than he needed air, to do something that would bind Mal to him, prove his worth in his eyes. Or perhaps it was a simple, selfish desire for more of Mal's touch.

"Do you think we might not have tried hard enough?" he asked, throat tight with nerves. "If, last night, if it helped him. And this morning too. It might be worthwhile to — to continue the experiment."

Tom couldn't bring himself to turn and look fully at Mal's face, but out of the corner of his eye he caught Mal's expression: something between eagerness and horror. Mal's shoulders tensed and his fists clenched.

His tone was almost too casual as he replied, "I don't see how it could hurt anything."

Tom's chest felt like it might burst from the force of his joy, his relief, his hope. They made the rest of the walk back to the house in silence, but this time it felt full of possibility.

Chapter Fourteen

WILLIAM'S BEDCHAMBER DOOR stood ajar, and Tom could hear the quiet murmur of voices: William's and Carter's, probably, but Tom could never mistake the low rumble of Mal's. He tried to shift his expression into something a little less like the beaming foolishness of a love-struck idiot, but the smile kept forcing its way back onto his face.

Tom pushed the door open and stepped inside anyway, shoving down a feeling uncomfortably close to shyness. Earlier in the morning Mal certainly wouldn't have welcomed his presence in William's sickroom, but now — now he felt he might be able to earn a place here, in this little family group. Gods, but he longed for that, the security of a welcome that would never be revoked. Such family life as he'd had in the past had always rested on lies, concealment, the knowledge that he was either already a disappointment or about to become one.

"Tom!" William called out cheerfully. "I was hoping you'd stop in to see me." William was propped up in bed. He was still resting on a mound of pillows and wrapped in a cocoon of blankets, but he had a little color in his cheeks.

At least that gave Tom an excuse for his ridiculous smile. "I didn't want to barge in on you until I was sure you were awake." Tom glanced quickly at Mal, seated in his usual chair by the bed. Mal sat a little stiffly, as if unsure how to react, but he didn't look unhappy to see him.

They had separated at the top of the stairs, both retiring to their own chambers to wash and dress. Tom could still feel the quick kiss Mal had pressed to his lips before he disappeared down the corridor.

"Awake, and in need of company," William said. "Mal won't read to me. He claims it's because my choice of literature bores him, but really it's that he won't wear his —"

Mal started bolt upright, his cheeks flaming. "For the gods' sakes —"

"Spectacles!" William finished triumphantly, and then burst into laughter.

Tom looked back and forth between the two of them, utterly gobsmacked. "Mal wears spectacles?"

"No, of course I bloody don't!" Mal put in, sounding disgusted.

William rolled his eyes. "No, he doesn't, but he *ought to*," he said, with a pointed glare at his cousin. "He's a little bit more vain than he is shortsighted, which is to say, a great deal."

Mal rose abruptly. "I'll leave you to read, then." He brushed by Tom without ceremony on his way out the door.

There was a short silence after his departure, William staring openmouthed after him. Tom wished he could sink through the floor. The last thing he'd wanted was to disturb them, and now he felt like more of an interloper than ever. At least he was no longer smiling.

"I should have known better than to twist his tail in front of you." William shook his head. "I didn't think."

"It doesn't matter," Tom said, not quite able to hide his bitterness.

"Don't look so downcast," William said gently. "I think it's rather sweet. Or would be, if Mal weren't such an idiot about showing when he cares for someone's good opinion."

Tom glanced up sharply at that, a rebuttal on the tip of his tongue — and then he remembered, almost too late, that he and Mal had agreed to let William believe they had married for love. It was far more likely that Mal simply objected to Tom being part of his family intimacy with his cousin. Mal, giving a damn whether Tom found his shortsightedness laughable, or unappealing in a lover? Not a chance.

"At least he can't criticize our choice of books," Tom ventured, forcing a weak smile.

The effort was enough for William, though, or at least he was willing to pretend it was. "True enough, he's a wet blanket. Where did we leave off?"

Nearly three hours passed before Tom looked up from the book for more than a sip of the tea Carter had set by his elbow soon after Tom sat down.

William was asleep, head tipped back and a faint smile on his face. Tom set the book on his chair and eased out of the room as quietly as he could. Carter, waiting patiently in the corridor, nodded at him and slipped by to take his place at William's bedside.

Tom went back to his own bedchamber, so eager to see Mal that he knew he mustn't give in to temptation. He would only act like a fool. Instead, he rang for a tray in his room so that he'd be able to miss dinner, and he hid there for the rest of the day.

WHEN THE CLOCK in the hall chimed half-past seven, Mal had to admit at last that Tom wasn't going to come down to dinner. His irritation was directly in proportion to the amount of time he'd spent dressing for the meal — and that was, he was forced to admit to himself, excessive. What could it matter? He was the same man — touchy, vain, unkind, and too quick to yield to temper — in his best coat and breeches as he was half-naked in the woods, taking Tom with too little consideration for the way he'd already had him the night before.

Mal winced at the memory of his own thoughtlessness. Tom had to be sore, but Mal had thought of nothing but how much he needed to forget himself in Tom's willing body. And he had been willing. Mal was sure of that. Mal was less certain that Tom cared enough for his own welfare to refuse, even if he ought to have.

For appearances' sake, Mal picked at his dinner, managing to eat a few bites and spread the rest around his plate before he pushed back from the table and strode out of the room. The cook would be offended, but Mal couldn't do more. The morsels he'd eaten sat in his belly like a lump of granite.

The library. He would sit in the library, drink a brandy, settle his nerves. The rest of the evening could be spent with Will. If Tom wanted to avoid him, he had the right.

Mal took the stairs two at a time and was knocking on

Tom's bedchamber door within seconds. When no answer came, Mal simply turned the knob and pushed the door open, letting it swing wide.

There was no one there, and not a single candle was lit. Mal's heart gave an agonizing squeeze and his vision blurred. Tom had gone. Tom had snuck down the back stairs, left Maberley, left *Mal* — and then he saw Tom's gold-limned chestnut hair peeking out of the top of the bedding, just barely gleaming in the faint firelight.

Mal could breathe again, and he did, a great heaving lungful that left him nearly as lightheaded as before. Tom had only fallen asleep. And he hadn't woken when Mal entered the room. Something about that unconscious trust, the way Tom felt safe enough in this house with him to fall asleep so deeply, twisted Mal up inside.

Careful not to make another sound, he closed the door, pulled off his shoes and set them aside, and then skinned out of his coat and draped it over a chair. The hush in the room was absolute; the rain had held off all day, and no sound filtered in from the rest of the house. Maberley could almost have been under a spell, like the one that had befallen the Beauty of the fairy-tale — and Mal the prince come to break it. He smiled at the thought. He was hardly a prince.

That didn't mean he couldn't wake Tom with a kiss. Mal crept closer, until he could lean over Tom and gently pull back the blanket from around his head. Tom was facing away, and the curve of his soft cheek was all Mal could reach. It was flushed from sleep, faintly pinpricked with golden stubble, and altogether too lovely for words. Perhaps a kiss on the lips was more traditional, but Mal was quite satisfied with pressing his mouth to the angle of Tom's jaw, nuzzling under to reach his throat.

Tom stirred and made a sleepy murmur that shot straight to Mal's prick. "Tom," he whispered. And then, helplessly, "Tom."

The flavor of his skin burst on Mal's tongue like the rarest delicacy, and he followed the line of Tom's throat to the curve of his shoulder, carefully pulling the coverlet down to expose him inch by inch. Tom's soft moans set his nerves blazing, every extremity tingling as if it were him waking, and for the first time. Mal wanted to drown in him, sink into him and never emerge. He worked his hands down Tom's body, tracing every sleep-warm contour of him before wrapping one hand firmly around his cock.

Mal slid onto the bed behind Tom, curling around him and stroking him off with steady precision. He sucked a mark onto Tom's shoulder, right over a tantalizing freckle, and reveled in the sounds he drew out of his lover and the way Tom's sinuous movements pressed his arse back against Mal's groin.

"You can," Tom stuttered. "Mal. You can. Oh goddess, you can do what you please with me..."

That was almost more than Mal could bear, and he thrust against Tom's arse involuntarily. "This is what I please," he growled into Tom's neck, and he caught a mouthful of soft skin and worried it between his lips. Tom groaned and spilled all over Mal's hand, his body shaking and his head thrown back.

Mal stroked him through the aftershocks, soothing the marks he'd left with gentle swipes of his tongue. His cock was ramrod-straight, pressed between Tom's cheeks, but he felt no urgent need for his own release. This was enough: the feel of Tom pliant in his arms, and the knowledge that he had, for once, given more than he had taken. It was more than enough. Certainly, it was more than Mal deserved.

"I meant it, you know," Tom all but purred. He stretched lazily, rubbing his arse up and down in a way that made Mal clench his teeth and cling to his good intentions by the tips of his fingers. "You can have me."

"Not three times in less than twenty-four hours," Mal gritted out. "I don't need to finish. Not now."

"Mmm," Tom murmured. "But perhaps I need you to."

He twisted about until his face was a bare inch from Mal's and their bodies were flush from chest to thigh, and he grinned, his eyes gleaming with desire and mischief. Mal had seen Tom play the seducer, had seen him mocking and cruel, lustful and lost in pleasure.

But this Tom — open, playful, happy, and truly *wanting* — this Tom devastated every last atom of Mal's resistance. No man could be expected to see Tom like this and do anything but prostrate himself in abject worship.

Mal leaned in and kissed Tom as he never had yet, teasing each curve of his lips and savoring every recess of his mouth.

"Far be it from me to deny you anything," he said, when their lips finally separated. And he meant it, probably far more than Tom would ever know.

Tom gazed at him for a moment, eyes wide and lips curved into a smile that held a thousand secrets. "Lie back, then, and don't argue."

Mal laughed breathlessly and rolled onto his back. "How well you know me — oh *fuck*, Tom —" Tom dipped his head and closed his lips over Mal's erection, mouthing over the fabric of his trousers. "Believe me," he gasped, "I'm not arguing."

Tom smiled up at him and tugged his buttons open. "I should hope not. But one never knows with you."

Mal dropped his head back against the pillow and buried his hands in Tom's thick hair, biting his lip to keep in a moan of sheer delight as Tom's tongue flicked over the head of his cock. There was no arguing that night.

Chapter Fifteen

THERE WAS PRECIOUS LITTLE arguing during the days that followed, and Tom began to suspect something was amiss with Mal. It seemed so unlike him, the way he humored Tom's every whim — sometimes playful, and sometimes earnest, but always indulgent and never unkind. It made Tom's heart ache. A cold, unfeeling Malcolm Leighton had been hazardous enough to Tom's peace of mind. This one would be fatal.

"A little lower," Tom gasped on the second night of their strange truce, tugging Mal's hair in an effort to shift him where Tom really wanted him.

Mal grinned up at him. "Like this?" He left off kissing Tom's stomach and moved to nibble at his hipbone.

"Ugh," Tom groaned, and then moaned at a higher pitch as Mal laughed and took Tom's cock fully down his throat in one motion. Tom lost himself in the now-familiar pleasure of it, the rough scrape of Mal's unshaven cheeks against his thighs, the grip of Mal's big hands pinning him so wonderfully in place, and more than anything, the hot pressure of Mal's talented and generous mouth.

It wasn't long at all before he lay sated, breath hitching in his chest, with Mal nuzzling at his hip again.

"I'll return the favor in just a moment," Tom said.

"Turn over and you won't need to do anything at all?"

That sounded like an even better idea, and Tom rolled over and let his legs fall open. "Wake me when you reach the interesting part," he said, and then laughed into the pillow as Mal's hand struck his arse and then lingered for a squeeze.

On the third night, Mal didn't get out of bed when they were finished, falling asleep curled around Tom's back with their fingers entwined and resting against Tom's chest. He was gone when Tom woke, but the sheets were still warm when he snuggled down to catch another hour's sleep.

That set the pattern; after that, Mal never went to his own room before Tom had fallen asleep. On the twelfth morning — not that Tom would have admitted to counting — he woke first. It was very early, still pre-dawn. A crack between the curtains let in the faintest tint of watery gray. Tom lay on his back, with Mal on his side with his arm draped over Tom's waist. The soft sounds of his breath mingled with the gentle patter of rain on the leaves of the spreading horse-chestnut whose branches nearly brushed Tom's windows.

Mal's black hair stuck up in all directions and he had faint creases on his cheek from the pillow; his mouth hung open just a little, most inelegantly.

He was by far the most beautiful thing Tom had ever seen.

Tom had tried to believe himself in love more than once; he had, to his shame, successfully convinced others of his love at least twice. Love wasn't something that came easily to him, and he'd come to think it would be some great revelation when it finally struck him, an epiphany that would leave him reeling from the shock of it. It would be the crest of a great wave of passion, and it would sweep him away.

Lying in bed with Mal on a damp and drizzly morning, love came to him like the gentle warmth of early spring sunshine after months of cold. It spread through his veins like honey, sweet and slow and soothing, filling him with nothing but contentment.

Mal had changed, and perhaps that didn't mean something was wrong after all; perhaps it simply meant that all was right. William's illness still haunted all of them, but he'd been stronger. Not improving any more than he had at first, but not declining, either. It was enough to give Tom hope, hope for all of them.

He would wait to speak to Mal, though — until William was truly better, and until he could be more certain of Mal's feelings. Tom could wait. They were married, something that sent a shiver of delight through him whenever he recalled it; he could wait.

Tom closed his eyes, wanting to at least appear to be sleeping when Mal woke. It didn't need to be this morning. He could wait.

THE THUMP OF THE HEAVY FRONT DOOR echoed through the hall, and a moment later Mal heard Tom's light tenor: a few cheerful words for the footman, a merry laugh. Mal closed his eyes a moment, trying to force down the anger he knew, or at least he *hoped*, was as unfair as it was irrational. Tom had done nothing wrong; he had tried his best.

And yet. And yet, if Tom had truly done his best, if

he'd obeyed Mirreith's plan for him, why hadn't she carried out her obligations? A blessing came with conditions, but its benefits were clear and absolute: good fortune, good health, and an assurance that the family would continue.

If Will died, they would have none of those. And he would die, there was no longer any doubt of that.

The library door opened to admit Tom, pink-cheeked and smiling, bearing with him a waft of the freshness of the lake and the first greenery of spring.

"Mal! Henry said you were in here. There's a path on the other side of the lake..." Tom's smile slipped as he took in Mal's expression. Mal hadn't looked in a mirror, but he hardly needed to; he could feel the weight of his own scowl, the tension of frustration and impotent rage in his limbs. "Mal? What's the matter?"

"Dr. Porter's just gone. Will's going to be dead by morning." Mal forced the words out flatly, taking a savage, self-destructive pleasure in making them as blunt as he could manage. Just the thought of it tore at his soul, but causing Tom some of the suffering he deserved would ease the pain. It must.

But instead of satisfaction, all Mal felt as Tom's face crumpled in horror was disgust. For himself, and his idiotic plan; for Tom, and his inability to do even this one damn thing right; for the whole world, for Mirreith, for all the gods and their cruelty.

He turned away and braced himself against the fireplace mantel, sucking in deep breaths and trying to banish the dark spots swirling in his vision.

"How is that possible? He was better." Tom's faint

voice was hardly audible over the humming in Mal's ears and in his mind. "It's been almost a fortnight since we —"

"Since I deluded myself into thinking that buggering you would serve a purpose?" Mal asked harshly. Behind him, Tom made a quiet, gut-punched sound. Good. Let him feel it. "And now he'll be dead within hours and I'll have the satisfaction of knowing I spent his last weeks on this earth fucking you rather than carrying out my responsibilities. Rather than comforting the only person I've ever loved —" His voice broke at last.

Only the drumming of his own heartbeat filled the silence, though his anger rose and rose, choking him with the pressure. It must have an outlet. Mal turned again. Tom stood precisely where he had when Mal had looked away, as still and white and graven as a marble statue.

"Well?" he demanded. Tom's lips moved, but no sound emerged. "Nothing to say? No empty platitudes?"

"What happened?" Tom finally whispered. "This morning, when I looked in on him — he was just as usual."

This morning, when Mal had woken as usual, tangled up with Tom in his bed, Tom's rumpled hair and lazy smile Mal's first sight of the day. This morning, when Tom had brushed an affectionate kiss over Mal's cheek before setting off to say hello to Will and then ramble the grounds for a few solitary hours.

"He had another fit. It lasted seven minutes as far as Carter and I could time it. And he hasn't woken." Mal aimed each word as he would a weapon. "Dr. Porter says he won't."

Tom nodded slowly, and his jaw tightened. "He could be wrong."

"He isn't. We both know it." Mal glanced over at the brandy decanter. He could drink the whole of it, and it wouldn't be enough. Mal could resist the temptation of it for now; he might have wasted Will's last weeks, but he'd remain sober now and pray for the chance to say goodbye before the end. By tomorrow he'd have nothing left but the brandy, anyway.

Because Will would be gone, and after that there would be no reason for Tom to stay. Not that Mal would want him to, dammit.

"Don't," Tom said. "That won't help."

And damn Tom for reading him so easily, for still standing there, so pale and apparently grief-stricken, as though Will were anything to him. "As if you give a fuck what I do," Mal snarled. "I'll ask the temple for a divorce decree when I go tomorrow to fetch a priestess for Will's rites. Save me a second visit. And then you won't need to pretend to be concerned."

"I'm not pretending!" Tom's voice rang out loudly in the hushed room. "Do you think you don't matter to me? That — that William doesn't matter to me? He wouldn't want you to —"

"And you're the authority on what's in Will's mind, are you? Besides, he thinks —" Mal took a deep, shuddering breath. "He *thought* we loved one another. At least he'll die believing I had something more than a bottle to comfort me. That's something, I suppose."

"You do," Tom said quietly. "You do. Mal, I love you."

Time seemed to stop for a moment, even the clock on the shelf in the corner pausing in its ticking. Grief already had its claws so deeply in Mal that it took him that suspended instant to understand the sensation welling up in him as pain, fresh and vivid and overwhelming.

Tom gazed at him, blue eyes wide and limpid, all false innocence and feigned sincerity. "Go to the devil," Mal choked out. "Get out of this house."

Tom flinched, but he stepped forward, never looking away. "I love you. I don't want a divorce, I don't want to leave you." Mal backed away, quickly. If Tom came close enough to touch, he might — do anything at all, from throwing him on the floor and taking him to knocking him down. Tom's tone took on a tinge of panic. "I thought I could wait to tell you, wait to see if you felt the same way. But now I can't wait. Please, will you say something? Anything at all?"

"Perhaps I should ask your former fiancé how he responded. Or your former wife. Or any of the other dupes you've left in your wake." And that was all he was: another fool. "I don't believe a word out of your mouth. I should thank them for allowing me to learn from their mistakes."

Tom stopped and closed his eyes, his throat working as he swallowed. When his eyelids fluttered open again, his lashes shone with unshed tears. "Please," he said, very low. "Please believe me. I wanted to love them. I treated them both badly, and I know I can never atone for it, but *I love you*. I could never tell either of them the truth, but I haven't anything to hide from you. You know who I truly am."

"A liar," Mal ground out. Because Tom was a liar — self-confessed, and until this moment, when it was convenient, seemingly unrepentant. Believing anything else would be the act of a delusional idiot, no matter how Tom's sky-blue eyes shone, no matter how sweet his kisses or how his laughter warmed even the coldest night. "An accomplished liar at that."

"I'm begging you," Tom said, and yes, that was panic, bright and sharp in every syllable and in every angle of his posture. "Please, I'll..." He looked about him wildly. And then he dropped to his knees, not even seeming to notice the painful-sounding thud as they struck the oak floorboards. "I'll do anything. I'll — I'll *be* anything, for you. Just don't send me away."

It was like a knife to the chest. Everything Mal could ever want, and Tom was asking him, *begging* him, to simply take it. Will would be gone. Mal's life wouldn't matter to anyone, and if he wanted to spend it lavishing his hopeless passion on a man who desired him for his fortune and for a refuge from the world, who would stop him? Mal allowed himself a dizzying vision of his future: Tom in his arms, Tom on his knees, joy in sorrow and laughter through his tears.

And the inevitable betrayal when Tom's nature could no longer be repressed even for Mal's well-padded pocketbook, and he took a lover, or a mistress, or three of each. Mal would find them in his own bed, perhaps, or Tom would stumble in late after an evening engagement with his cravat hanging loose and his trousers partly buttoned, with a shrug and a glib excuse and the scent of another man's body clinging to his.

How many times would Mal forgive him, sickened by his own weakness but sicker still with the fear of losing even the crumbs of affection Tom offered to humor him?

"I want nothing from you," Mal said heavily, a lie as great as any of Tom's. One more moment in that room, thinking of what he could do to Tom as he knelt there, and Mal would lose his resolution. He strode across the library and dodged the arm Tom flung out to stop him. At the threshold he turned; Tom's head hung down, buried in his hands.

Mal stepped into the hall and shut the door firmly behind him. He would go to Will's bedside and sit his solitary vigil. Mal had neglected him enough; he would not allow him to die alone.

Chapter Sixteen

THE LIBRARY DOOR SHUTTING behind Mal had the finality of a death knell. Tom stayed where he was, knees aching and tears flowing down his cheeks behind his hands to gather in the dip of his collarbones.

Time passed, hours perhaps. The house lay in absolute quiet, but it was the claustrophobic hush of grief and fear bottled up until the pressure became almost a sound of its own. The sun had come out during the morning and it slanted across Tom's face, shining in his eyes for a little while and then fading away as it passed him by.

Tom came back to himself with a start to the sound of wheels on the drive and knelt bolt upright, heart pounding like a kettledrum and sweat pooling horridly along his spine. He gazed around him dully, the familiar furnishings of the library alien and distant. The library clock told him it was a quarter past four. It must be Dr. Porter returning.

Climbing to his feet was more difficult than he expected, his stiff joints protesting every motion. Tom focused on each individual ache. So long as he felt only that, he could block out the rest.

Voices in the hall caught his attention. One was Anderson, William's butler, but there were two others, both male but neither of them the doctor or Mal.

A twisting bolt of misery and anger and betrayal shot

through Tom at the thought of Mal, but he forced it aside. Of course Mal had reacted that way; anyone would have. That not even the sight of Tom begging on his knees had been enough to sway him told Tom all he needed to know about Mal's feelings. There was nothing there to hope for. Tom would stay until William was dead, and then — as Mal had told him to do, and as he had no choice but to do — he would go to the devil. Tom hardly cared what that might mean in practical terms.

The voices swelled, Anderson's growing a little frantic. Tom caught Mal's name, and his hackles rose; one of the visitors sounded familiarly unpleasant. Before he could identify him the conversation grew muffled and then faded away completely, as if the group had gone into one of the rooms that opened from the hall.

William lay unconscious and dying upstairs and Mal was no doubt with him. No matter how cruelly Mal had rejected him, Tom couldn't allow them to be disturbed; it was a matter of common decency. He was no doubt disheveled and tear-stained, but there was no help for it. He hadn't the time to go upstairs and put himself to rights, not if he wished to head off Anderson from fetching Mal out of sheer necessity.

Tom followed the faint sounds through the hall and into the drawing room, which was rarely used, at least since Tom had come to the house. William hadn't been receiving calls for quite some time, and Mal didn't make himself at home to guests while at Maberley.

He opened the door and stopped on the threshold, blinking in the hope that what he saw might vanish when he opened his eyes again.

No such luck. Marcus Leighton stood before the fireplace, brandy in hand, and beside him was another gentleman Tom had never seen before. Anderson was arranging more glasses on the sideboard. Marcus stared for a moment and then let out an unpleasant bark of laughter, his lips twisted into a sneer.

"So," he barked, before Tom could gather his wits. "It's true. When I heard Mal married you I didn't believe it. I couldn't credit that he would lower himself to this, but here you are."

Marcus's companion looked Tom up and down, an openly lascivious survey that would have been discourteous if directed at a whore on the street. He was just the sort of man Tom might have chosen for a quick fuck in the back of a gentleman's club in the past: tall, and blond, and handsome in the way men like that could be before drink and debauchery blurred the edges of their good looks. Now, the thought of his touch made Tom's flesh crawl, and his gaze was nearly as bad.

"Come now, Leighton," the man drawled. "At least your cousin doesn't settle for second-rate goods."

"Might have been a prime article a few years back, but he's used goods now," Marcus replied. He lifted his glass to his thick lips, malice glinting in his eyes as he stared Tom down over the rim of it.

Out of the corner of his eye, Tom could see that Anderson had gone utterly still, frozen in the act of brushing a speck of dust from a decanter with a cloth. Marcus and his bloody guest had spoken as if Anderson wasn't even there — as if Tom were a servant himself.

Tom was accustomed to this type of treatment,

particularly since his family had cast him out. But he wasn't that man anymore, wasn't Tom Drake, penniless outcast and social pariah. At least for the moment — and as far as Marcus knew, permanently — he was Thomas Drake-Leighton, the husband of an honorable and respectable man, and he had more standing in this household than Marcus Leighton did. Marcus might be a cousin to Mal and William, but while William lay ill this was Mal's household. Until Mal divorced him this was *their* household.

Rage rose up, nearly choking him, but he tamped it down and forced himself to calm. He was the master here, and he would bloody well act like it. Mal might not thank him for it and might not even care how Marcus spoke to him. But he'd be damned if he'd take this in what was, for now at least, his own home.

He lifted his chin and looked down his nose at Marcus's companion, giving him much the same sort of examination he'd just received. "Who the devil are you?" he asked coldly.

The stranger and Marcus exchanged a quick glance, and Tom hid a smile. Ignoring their insults entirely clearly hadn't been his expected response.

"Anderson," Tom said briskly into the silence, "apprise Mr. Leighton of these gentlemen's presence in the house." He put a slight sardonic emphasis on *gentlemen* and had the satisfaction of seeing Marcus flush a dull brick-red. "Don't disturb anyone unduly," he added, hoping Anderson would show a little discretion. Marcus need not know how close to the brink of death William had gone. Tom had learned that Anderson wasn't the quickest study on his first day at Maberley, and he prayed that the fellow could at least take a hint now, when it mattered. "And send to the stables to let them know that the horses should be fed and watered but not put up. They'll be needed again within the hour."

"You'll do no such thing!" Marcus cried. "You'll ready two bedchambers at once, and tell Mal —"

"Tell me what?" Tom had never been so glad to hear anyone's voice. Such relief at Mal standing right behind him was shameful, after the way he had spoken to Tom earlier, but he couldn't help himself. Goddess, if only Mal would take his part.

"That your catamite's acting the lord of the manor," Marcus snapped. That word brought bile rushing up into Tom's throat, but the shock of it jarred him out of his anger for a moment, long enough to look at Marcus, really look. His face was florid with — not with offense, as Tom had thought a moment before. There was something else there, something in his eyes. A calculating, watchful something.

He glanced at Marcus's companion, catching the ghost of a smirk before it vanished. Something was wrong here, very wrong indeed. Anxiety prickled down his spine. He had to pull Mal aside, out of this room, and quickly.

"He may take your cock like the practiced whore he is," Marcus was saying. "But I assure you he'd moan like a lightskirt for any man who wanted to bend him over —"

Mal pushed roughly past, and Tom caught at his sleeve. "Mal, don't —" But it was too late. The brandy glass shattered on the floor in a burst of sparkling shards, and Marcus fell back, catching himself on the mantel before he fell into the fireplace. Marcus's hand flew to his face, crimson dripping between his fingers. Mal took a step back, fist still raised, knuckles smeared with Marcus's blood.

Marcus's friend didn't so much as twitch, but a slow, malicious smile spread across his face. "Oh, bloody well done," he said to Mal, and then turned to Marcus. "You'll need satisfaction for that, I expect."

Tom could almost see the pieces falling into place, faster and faster, like dominoes set up along a slope. William dying. Marcus, William's heir, and William, Mal's heir. If William died first, Mal could always make arrangements to leave his property elsewhere, or he could marry again and have children, but if Mal died first, William would legally possess his entire estate and it would quickly pass to Marcus. Mal's shortsightedness, something Marcus would surely know, and which would give Mal a near-insuperable handicap with a pistol. And Tom, the easy target for Marcus's insults — insults that no husband could leave unanswered, even if he agreed with the substance of them.

It passed through his mind in a flash, and he stepped forward as Marcus was still opening his mouth to reply. He couldn't be allowed to; once a challenge was issued, there was no way out. Tom had only one available choice.

"Not until I have mine," he said.

Marcus's rapidly purpling face might have been amusing under other circumstances, passing as it did from disbelief to horror to rage. "No! No, I don't think — I've been struck!" he blustered. "That takes priority over any —"

"The hell it does." Tom felt control flowing back to

him, perversely stimulated by Marcus's lack of it. "You called me a whore, used goods, a catamite, and a lightskirt, I believe," he went on, enunciating each word with great precision.

"And as your husband, I took exception," Mal cut in. "There won't be any satisfaction given, this is absurd —"

"There most certainly will be satisfaction," exclaimed Marcus's friend, with some heat. "You attacked him in a way no gentleman could ignore —"

"I can't allow such an insult to pass without taking it up, damn you —"

"Be silent!" Tom shouted. "All of you shut your bloody mouths!" The other three trailed off after a moment, staring at Tom as if he'd grown a second head. "Mr. Leighton," Tom said to Marcus, "I demand satisfaction for your insults to my good name. Unless you're too much a coward, we'll meet tonight."

"You will not!" Mal seized Tom by the arm and yanked him close, until their faces were only a few inches apart. Mal's eyes blazed with some emotion Tom couldn't identify, something that made him want to fall to his knees all over again. And then Mal said the only words that could have snapped Tom out of his instinctive desire to do as Mal asked. "As your husband, I forbid it."

"No," Tom replied. And then, with more force, "The hell you do." Few of Tom's father's lessons had been meant to help him, and even fewer had done so. But Tom was a man, his own man, something Mr. Drake had always insisted upon. He could shoot, and well; he knew his own mind. And no husband would take that from him.

Mal's hand tightened convulsively around his bicep.

"Tom, don't do this. You can't do this —"

Tom pulled his arm decisively from Mal's grasp and turned back to Marcus, away from Mal's pleading look. He was his own man, but he wasn't made of stone, either. "Well? Do you accept? It matters little to me either way, but make up your mind."

Marcus and his friend exchanged a look, both of them appearing equally chagrined. Tom had preempted them, and they both knew it.

"I accept," Marcus said with a sneer. "Your wrist's too limp to hold up a pistol in any case."

Mal surged forward again, but this time Marcus's companion intercepted him, blocking his access to Marcus. "Don't. You and I have a duel to arrange, presuming we're the seconds."

Mal's fists clenched by his sides, but after moment he nodded stiffly and took a step back. He looked ready to do murder, and Tom had never seen him so pale and set.

"Well, then," Tom said, with a nonchalance he hoped covered the frantic pounding of his heart, "we'd best send for Dr. Porter. And get this over with."

Chapter Seventeen

"THIS IS MADNESS," Dr. Porter grumbled. "Utterly insane. With my patient sure to be dead by morning, must we really add to the count of corpses?"

They stood side by side at the edge of a small lawn set far enough from the back of the house to be out of direct view of the windows, but close enough to carry a man inside if he were unconscious. Or dead, as Dr. Porter so tactlessly predicted. Marcus stood a little ways away, muttering to himself, while Tom paced on Mal's other side. Mal had already examined the pistols, a matched pair that Will kept in a case on the wall of his study. Mr. Thorpe, Marcus's second, was now engaged in the same, and he set the second gun down in its case with a slow nod of approval.

Dr. Porter was right. This was madness. There was something to it, though, that transcended even Marcus's preternatural ability to offend and Tom's reckless inability to control his impulses. It teased at the edges of Mal's mind, just eluding comprehension.

Mal gritted his teeth and glanced over at Tom. Thorpe had drawn out the process of choosing suitable ground and arranging the angle of the combatants almost to the point of deliberate obstruction. He'd argued first that they couldn't possibly be perpendicular lest the sun shine directly in one duelist's eyes, and then that they couldn't possibly be parallel because they would of course each turn to the side to present a smaller target, and thus one would be disadvantaged again.

All the while, Mal couldn't forget for a moment that Will was dying, upstairs with only Carter to keep watch over him. Each second of wasted time felt like another fresh wound, cut upon cut.

In the end, just when Mal's grip on his temper frayed beyond repair, Tom snapped that he would take the side that had him facing the sun when he turned to fire, and he didn't give a bloody damn, as he wished to fight before the sun went down entirely.

Had that been Thorpe's intent from the beginning, to draw things out until the fight must be postponed? It was odd indeed. He'd been eager enough to push Marcus into challenging Mal, after all.

And he had nearly succeeded in delaying past the point where a duel could take place. A few clouds were beginning to drift in from the north. For now the light held, rust-red and gloomy but enough for the purpose, but that would only last another quarter of an hour at the most. Tom was clearly still impatient, his foot tapping. But his gaze was fixed on Marcus, not on Thorpe.

Dr. Porter left Mal's side to approach Marcus, who was standing a few yards away. "Mr. Leighton," he said, his voice carrying clearly. "Will you not reconsider and apologize to Mr. Drake-Leighton? A fight like this, while one of your nearest relatives lies so close to death, is hardly fitting."

"Will's been dying for months," Marcus remarked, so

unconcerned that Mal had to hold himself back from trying again to break his face.

"Some of us held out hope," Dr. Porter said, in the frostiest tone Mal had ever heard from the man. "In any case, such hope as there was is now gone, and Mr. Leighton will also be gone by morning. I reiterate, this is far from fitting."

The extraordinary change that came over Marcus's face was riveting. Smug, sneering indifference transformed in an instant into an almost feral desperation.

"By morning?" Marcus stammered. It could almost have been mistaken for the shock of grief if Marcus hadn't shown how little he cared for Will's life only moments before. "But he can't die before..."

Marcus shot a look at Thorpe, who grimaced and shrugged. "If you're free of this obligation," Thorpe hissed under his breath.

"Tom," Marcus said suddenly, his hands clenching and unclenching at his sides and his face unhealthily flushed. "I apologize."

Mal looked back and forth between Tom and Marcus and Thorpe, now more than ever certain he was missing something that the other three all seemed to understand.

Tom curled his lip, baring his teeth in a silent snarl. "I don't accept."

"Mr. Drake-Leighton," Dr. Porter cut in, "I beg you to reconsider."

At the same moment, Marcus cried, "Damn you, you must accept!"

"Not a chance," Tom shot back. "You'll fight *this challenge* and no other, and you won't be fit for more until

William's gone, I promise you —"

Tom cut himself off abruptly, flashing an anxious look at Mal. It was more than enough for the vile truth to break upon him. Mal had never liked Marcus, and associated with him only occasionally out of family solidarity. But he'd stood by him through mounting debts, a scandal involving a merchant's wife, a rumor of cheating at cards, and a whole raft of smaller peccadilloes. Naively, he'd believed himself the recipient of a similar loyalty.

That Marcus could plot to kill him in order to inherit his fortune along with Will's estate seemed like a deranged fantasy, the sort of scurrilous nonsense one would laugh at if one heard it said of an acquaintance.

But nothing else explained his sudden distress on hearing of Will's final hours, nor Thorpe's desire to promote a fight with Mal but not with Tom, nor — Tom. Tom, who had put it all together long before Mal had, and had chosen to take the duel on himself, to risk his own life rather than see Mal do the same.

Mal's eyes stung and his throat closed. Gods, what had he done?

"Mr. Leighton," Thorpe said. "Your assistance please?" It jerked Mal out of his shock and horror, and he turned to see Thorpe holding the pistol case.

Mal was Tom's second, and Tom had already refused his opponent's direct apology. There was nothing to be done but to cross the short distance that separated him from Thorpe, to stand mutely beside him as Tom and Marcus chose their weapons. Mal and Thorpe had already paced off the distance. That left Mal with only the time it would take to escort Tom to his mark.

"You can still accept his apology," he urged, keeping his voice low. "It's not too late to —"

"To be a coward?" Tom demanded, eyes flashing. "I may have nearly every fault known to humanity, but that's not bloody well one of them!"

Gods damn it, Mal had one chance at this, and he'd already misspoken. "To not sacrifice yourself for me," he said, voice thick with emotion he couldn't possibly repress. "Marcus is my cousin, my problem, not yours." Tom's mouth hung open in a silent *Oh*. "Accept his apology. Let him challenge me. This isn't your fight, Tom."

A flash of pain so bright and searing Mal nearly felt it in his own breast passed through Tom's eyes. "We won't be married much longer, no matter the outcome of this. But for now — just for today — I'm your husband. It's my problem too." Tom swallowed hard. In a near-whisper he added, "And I'm proud of it."

Mal would have signed his fortune over to Marcus for one single kiss from Tom's soft lips. Impossible, to make such a display at the moment; impossible to send Tom into the fight even more distracted than he was. Instead, he squeezed Tom's shoulder and stepped back to take his place to the side, feeling that he tore out his own heart as he did so.

Since neither Mal nor Thorpe trusted the other, they had asked Dr. Porter to drop the handkerchief to signal the start of the duel. The doctor stood scowling on the other side of the combatants, with Thorpe in position to Mal's right, nearer to Marcus.

Mal looked only at Tom, unable to tear his eyes away. The last rays of the setting sun over the trees behind Dr.

Porter gilded Tom's hair and lit his fair skin with pink. He stood ramrod-straight, chin up, facing Marcus with calm, steady courage.

Prayer had always seemed absurd to Mal. The gods would do as they wished, and he'd be buggered if he moped about like a wallflower at a dance attempting to catch their attention.

Mal didn't just pray, as he waited for the handkerchief to fall. He begged. He promised Mirreith anything, everything, his life's blood, if only Tom could live and be happy.

"Are you ready, gentlemen?" Dr. Porter asked, his voice rasping oddly in the stillness of the clearing.

Tom nodded, and Marcus growled, "Get on with it, then."

Dr. Porter waited a long moment, the white scrap of his handkerchief stained red as blood by the setting sun, and then he let it fall.

Marcus raised his arm first, his lips drawn back in a rictus of a smile. He'd always been a fair shot, and for all his bluster he wasn't one to succumb to nerves. Tom lifted his pistol more slowly but more deliberately, his lean body twisted to the side; he made a smaller target than Marcus, who had a gut beneath his waistcoat.

A deafening double report rang out, cracking through the clearing and echoing off the trees. A great flock of birds whirled up, flapping and screeching in deafening chorus. Tom's arm wavered, his knees buckled, and Mal was at his side before he knew he'd begun to run. Mal caught Tom around the waist and fell to his knees, Tom's full weight bringing them both down.

"Tom," Mal said, hardly able to hear his own voice over the ringing in his ears. The sharp scent of gunpowder overlaid the freshness of damp grass, but beneath that was the nauseating, richly metallic scent of fresh blood. "Tom, are you —" And he cut off with a choked cry as he turned Tom over and saw the stain seeping through the shoulder of his coat, black against the dark blue of the fabric. "Dr. Porter!" he cried out hoarsely.

Distantly, he heard Thorpe also calling for the doctor, and Marcus's foul oaths. Marcus was hit, then, but conscious. Mal didn't care one way or the other. He could see nothing but Tom's hauntingly beautiful face, white to the lips and far too still. Tom's head tipped back on Mal's arm was lifelessly heavy.

Hands pulled at Mal's arm, and a strident voice sounded in his ear. Dr. Porter. Mal moved one arm away, easing Tom down so that he lay on the ground but was still supported against Mal's chest.

Mal jumped as Dr. Porter let out a long, shrill whistle. Two of the footmen appeared a moment later, running down from the direction of the house.

"Well, one of us had to think ahead," Dr. Porter growled, not pausing in the act of packing a wad of gauze against Tom's shoulder. "You!" he called out. "Yes, you. Assist the other gentlemen. And you, lad, take his feet. Gently now, slow and gentle…"

Mal let himself be prodded into position, carefully supporting Tom's body, and between the three of them they lifted him and began to move toward the house, with Dr. Porter keeping pressure on Tom's wound as they walked.

"Will he," Mal caught his breath. "Will he live?"

"Don't ask me," Dr. Porter gasped, stumbling a little. "I'm just the doctor. Ask your bloody goddess."

I already have, for all the good it's done any of us, Mal thought bitterly. *But please. Please.*

Chapter Eighteen

THE FIRST SENSATION to return was Tom's hearing. His eyelids felt like lead weights, and his body was a distant, numb thing, hardly worth bothering about. Did he have a body? But he must have ears, for he could hear a faint voice, no louder than a whisper. It was familiar, but he couldn't make out the words — although he almost thought he discerned his own name, amongst the nonsense.

He drifted, and when he came back again there was nothing but pain, a searing, throbbing misery that filled his consciousness and seemed to come from everywhere at once and envelop his entire being.

There were more voices, and then something at his lips. It was bitter, so very bitter, and though he desperately tried to turn his head and spit it out someone held his head in place and forced him to drink.

Tom woke from time to time, never able to open his eyes more than a crack. The pain was sometimes dulled but always there. Once he saw William, his brows drawn together in a frown but his cheeks rosy and eyes bright — and he was standing, leaning over Tom and speaking to him, though his voice was muddled and indistinct as if heard from under water. William was dead. If William was dead, then Tom was too, and doubtless damned.

Panic surged over him, and he thrashed like a madman. Something pulled, and the pain became excruciating. He screamed, and William called out, and then there was more bitterness in his mouth. The darkness encroached again.

At last he drifted back up, and this time he could hear and feel clearly. His shoulder hurt, but it was more of a dull ache than the piercing agony of before. The rest of him felt heavy and weak, but his limbs rested between soft fabric and his head lay on a down pillow, by the softness cradling his skull. He must be alive. William, then, had been a dream, conjured by whatever fever had laid Tom low.

Somewhere nearby, a fire was burning; Tom could hear the soft pops and hisses of wood that had been laid on a little damp. And then there was the faintest rustling whisper — the page of a book being turned.

It took a moment of gathering his strength to force his eyes open, and then another to turn his head in the direction of the sound.

In an armchair by the bed sat — another illusion, it had to be. For it was Mal, unshaven and in his shirtsleeves, one stockinged ankle propped on the opposite knee. A book lay open in his lap. And propped on the bridge of his nose was a pair of wire-rimmed spectacles.

At the slight sound of Tom's movement, Mal looked up from the book, which slipped down the gap between his legs and tumbled to the floor with a thump.

"Tom," Mal said faintly, and surged off the chair to fall to his knees by the bed. One shaking hand cupped the side of Tom's face. The spectacles slid down Mal's nose, and he tore them off with his other hand and flung them aside. "Tom, are you really awake this time?"

Speaking was too much effort. Tom tried, but he could manage only a tiny shift of his head.

Mal reached up to the nightstand for a glass of water. With infinite gentleness, he lifted Tom's head and helped him sip a little between his parched lips.

"Better?" Mal set the glass back, but he didn't pull away, looking down into Tom's eyes with something like hunger in his gaze — that and heartbreaking relief.

"Yes," Tom whispered. "What — how long?"

Mal stroked his thumb over Tom's cheek. "Three days. The wound wasn't too bad, but a little scrap of your coat was caught in it and caused an infection. You were fevered, and so weak I thought —" Mal swallowed hard. "Thank the gods."

The wound. Tom remembered firing his own gun, and then a shocking jolt, the impact of Marcus's pistol ball. After that, there was pain, and confusion, and little else.

"In the shoulder?" He couldn't seem to form complete thoughts, let alone coherent sentences.

Mal nodded, following along anyway. "You shot Marcus in the hand. Took off two of his fingers," he said, preempting Tom's next question. Tom tried and failed to prevent the smile that stretched his painfully chapped lips. No doubt his savage satisfaction was inappropriate, but that hadn't ever stopped him before.

An answering smile curved Mal's lips. Tom stared at that smile, at that wonderful mouth. How could Mal be smiling, when William was dead?

"Mal." Terror seized him at the prospect of asking, but

he couldn't go another moment without knowing. "William? He is — is he? I thought I saw him."

"You did," Mal replied, his smile broadening into an irrepressible grin. Tom's heart gave a lurch. "He's alive. And better every day."

"Thank the goddess," Tom breathed, his eyes fluttering shut. He took a moment to simply savor it, that all of this hadn't been for nothing after all. Mal was alive, and William was alive, and Tom — well, at least his being alive offered the benefit of allowing him to appreciate it. "How?"

"I don't know exactly," Mal said. "But my theory is that Mirreith wanted us to honor our vows. Love's in the vows, isn't it? Will was better that night. After you…" He trailed off awkwardly, clearing his throat. And Mal throwing his pitiful declaration back in his face again *hurt*, far more than the lingering pain of his wounded shoulder. "I need to fetch Dr. Porter," Mal muttered, and fled.

Tom lay back and closed his eyes again, wanting nothing so much as oblivion.

Dr. Porter bustled in and woke him shortly after, changing the dressing on Tom's shoulder with a great deal of angry grumbling and imprecations against young men with no common sense. "Although it'd make my work a great deal easier if all my patients were blessed," he added. "You shouldn't have survived this."

Tom could only nod, his stomach churning and his head aching.

When he woke again it was William by his bedside, sipping a cup of tea and holding a familiar book. By the angle of the light through the windows, it was late morning, and Tom blinked, trying to reorient himself. It had been night when he woke last, he was quite sure.

"Are you going to read to me?" Tom whispered.

A blinding smile broke out on William's face. "Turnabout is fair play." He set his tea down in favor of helping Tom sip from a glass of water. "How are you feeling?"

"I ought to be asking you that."

"Don't think we won't have words about it once you're recovered," William said, trying for sternness and failing. "But for now, it's enough that I'm feeling almost like my old self."

Tom's heart sank. Mal had told William the truth, then: that their marriage was a ploy, and probably that it would end as soon as Tom was well enough to leave. Glad as he was to see William, he felt Mal's absence as keenly as his healing wound — the only difference being that his shoulder would heal with time.

William called for Carter, now apparently Tom's nurse rather than William's, and between them they saw to the lowering necessities of tending a bedridden man. "Don't look so shamefaced," William said cheerfully. "After the months I spent in bed, do you really think I'm squeamish?"

That helped, and Tom was grateful. And he was glad that it wasn't Mal trying to render these services, sparing him yet another humiliation. He had to be glad, or his heart would break. Had Mal's presence by his bedside been a dream? Tom hadn't seen him since then, not even so much as a glimpse.

By the next evening, Tom was well enough to sit up and have a proper cup of tea and even a little solid food.

He thought he'd never be able to look at broth or gruel again. But by the time he'd finished he was hardly able to keep his eyes open. William took his dishes and tiptoed out, setting the door just a little ajar behind him.

When Tom woke, blinking into the near-darkness of the quiet room, Mal was there at last. He sat in the armchair all of Tom's visitors used, but he wasn't reading, or napping; instead, he sat with his elbows on his knees, head hanging down in an attitude of utter defeat.

Clearly, he would rather be anywhere else. Heart racing, Tom held as still as he could. This might be his only chance to see Mal again, to breathe the same air, to memorize the strong lines of his shoulders and the way his hair stood up in the back, as if Mal had been running his hands through it.

Tom must have made some small, betraying sound. Mal lifted his head and their eyes met. Tom nervously licked his lips, and Mal's gaze flicked down for a moment, tracing the movement. Tom wished he could be pleased by that — wished he could be happy that Mal desired him still, but it gave him nothing but a sick, empty feeling in the pit of his stomach. Tom could inspire lust in most women and a surprising number of men; he wasn't proud of it. To be *that* for Mal was worse than to be nothing at all.

"I'm sorry," Mal said hoarsely, and pushed himself up out of his chair. "I'll fetch Will."

Tom turned his head away to hide his misery, but it didn't matter; Mal had always been able to read him.

"Tom?" Mal had stepped closer, enough that Tom could almost feel the warmth of him and catch the fragrance of his soap and his skin. It was torture, to be so close. "Do you need Dr. Porter?"

"Don't take care of me," Tom choked out. "I don't want your pity."

"My pity?" Mal asked sharply. "Is that what you think?"

Tom couldn't turn, couldn't bear to see whatever annoyance or impatience Mal would have written on his face. "I know you're only taking your turn as my nursemaid so William can sleep. It's not necessary. I'll be all right alone."

There was a long, pregnant silence. "Tom," Mal said slowly. "I've been sleeping in the corridor outside your bedchamber. Or not sleeping. But I haven't gone so far that I couldn't hear you if you asked for me, and you haven't. Not once."

The pain and the reproach in those words were nearly more than Tom could stand. How dare he, how *dare* he take offense at that?

"Don't," Tom gritted out. "You were — more than clear. When I told you how I felt, you were clear. Damn you, you don't owe me anything for the duel, or for William's recovery." It was a struggle to get the words out. But he had to; he had to, because what if Mal was too honorable to follow through with his plans for a divorce now that the marriage had achieved what they'd hoped, now that Tom's unwanted, despised love had brought William back from the brink of death? That would be worse than anything, to be kept as Mal's unwanted burden, fucked now and then and otherwise ignored. "I didn't — I don't want —" Tom gasped into frustrated silence, his lungs unwilling to give him the breath he needed.

Mal took a deep breath of his own and squared his shoulders, a man gathering his courage if ever Tom had seen one. "You want *me*," he said. "Or you did. Have you changed your mind?" Changed his mind? As if he could. "Because I want you, and I'm yours for as long as you'll have me. The rest of my life. Please," and Mal's voice broke on the word. "Please don't tell me that I lost the only chance I had."

Tom's heart kicked up into an unsteady, galloping rhythm that pulsed through every limb. "You didn't believe me." He sounded like a child begging for reassurance after a scolding, and he hated it. He wished he could hate Mal for reducing him to it. "You should have believed me," he said, and that was better.

"Yes," Mal agreed. "I should have. And I'd deserve it if you wanted to be done with me. But I love you, Tom. I love you more than life itself and I won't let you go without a fight." His steady gaze held nothing back: his fear of Tom's rejection, his sincerity, and his determination.

Tom had lied often, and concealed himself with whatever he thought his family or friends or lovers would want to see. Confronted with Mal's utter openness, he had nothing left to hide behind. He was only Tom, stripped bare and utterly vulnerable. For the first time, he could endure it, the thought of being known so completely that he had no secrets left.

"Tom, please say something," Mal asked. No, begged, shamelessly, and those were *tears* standing in Mal's eyes — tears, for him, for love of him.

"I haven't the strength to put up a fight," Tom

whispered, fighting back tears of his own. He gave up and let them fall. "Not that I would anyhow."

"Liar," Mal said, but his voice held nothing but adoration, and his smile lit up every corner of Tom's heart. "And I'll take nothing but pleasure in winning when you do."

It was a long time before Tom could bring himself to speak again, the joy swelling up in him too powerful for expression. Mal leaned in and pressed his lips to Tom's in the softest, chastest of kisses — not a demand, but a promise.

Tom knew it was one they both would keep.

Epilogue

SIX MONTHS LATER

MAL CHOSE HIS MOMENT carefully. He couldn't bring it up at dinner, not when Will was there. Tom rarely assumed his brittle, too-charming mask these days, even when uncomfortable subjects were raised before others, but this might be a bridge too far. Wandering Maberley's woods often left Tom in a receptive mood, but Mal was terrified that Tom might simply run away if he had the open ground to do so.

Tempting to ambush him immediately after fucking him, but no. Mal wasn't the most sensitive of men, but even he knew that the news of his correspondence with Tom's estranged brother was not best broken while Tom lay gasping for breath with Mal still buried inside him.

Even if it was doubly tempting to bring it up before he untied Tom's wrists from the bedpost, when Tom couldn't land him a facer.

And so he waited until they'd washed up and settled into the bed half an hour later, Tom wrapped in seemingly every blanket in the house despite September's lingering warmth. Mal was sweating just looking at him, but he pulled Tom to lie against his chest anyway. Physical comfort wasn't essential; Tom, on the other hand, was necessary down to Mal's very bones. The lazy weight of him on Mal's shoulder, the easy, affectionate way Tom rested one arm over Mal's waist, the fragrance of Tom's hair and the softness of it tickling his chin. Mal still couldn't forgive Mirreith for nearly letting Tom die, but he could admit that she'd shown good taste when she put her mark on him.

"What is it?" Tom asked, sounding not quite sleepy enough. "You may as well confess whatever it is you've been hiding from me all day."

Damn it. Mal hadn't quite worked out a plan for easing into the subject, and now he was the one caught in an ambush.

"It was meant to be a surprise," he hedged. "I'd meant to..." Ease Tom into it, though he wasn't sure how.

"You had a letter." Tom now sounded not sleepy at all. "This morning. And you've been odd ever since. You took it in the library to read instead of looking at it during breakfast as you usually do with the post."

Tom levered himself up and pushed away. The few inches between them felt like a yawning chasm. Mal reached out, and Tom pulled back further, staring down at his hands.

"You went to the city without me. Last month, you said I needn't go if I had rather stay and enjoy the weather," Tom said, with a quaver in his voice, a hesitancy he hadn't shown in months. "You had a letter then too, just before, that you didn't show me," he finished, so quietly Mal had to lean closer to make it out.

All at once, Mal understood. It was just like this that Tom had betrayed his former fiancé's trust — running off supposedly on urgent business and really meeting his mistress or his lovers. Before Mal knew his husband as well as he did now, Tom's suspicions would have driven him to a flight of temper. He would have assumed that Tom saw in him what he saw in himself, and he would have suspected Tom of infidelity.

Now he knew damn well how Tom thought, and it all but broke his heart to realize Tom still believed himself unworthy of better treatment.

"Sweetheart, it's not that," Mal said, with absolute firmness. "Look at me." He tipped Tom's head up with a finger beneath his chin until he could see Tom's eyes, dimmed with worry but as lovely as ever. "The letter I had before I went away was from my solicitor, and you can look at it as often as you like, for all the pleasure it will give you. I spent every moment of that journey missing you." That earned him a faint smile, and Mal couldn't resist leaning in to kiss it.

"Mmm," Tom said as Mal lifted his head at last. "I missed you too. And I'll want more of that in a moment. But explain yourself first."

Mal took a deep breath. "The letter this morning was from Arthur." Mal tensed, braced for Tom's response, but Tom only stared at him. "Arthur Drake, your brother."

Tom jerked back, twisting away from Mal's hand where it lay on his shoulder. "I know who Arthur is, you twat," he snapped, as bright red bloomed across his cheekbones, a sure sign of trouble. "What the devil do you mean by getting a letter from him? Is this the first?" At Mal's guilty wince, Tom all but shouted, "It's not the first! What the bloody hell are you playing at that you —"

"He wrote to me!" Mal shouted over him. "And yes, I replied, because you can pretend not to care all you like, but I know you miss him. I know you love him."

"You don't know anything," Tom snarled. "He never wants to see me again. And the feeling is entirely mutual."

"I know that's not true, because I know how I'd feel if it were me and Will."

"Oh?" Tom's lips twisted into a sneer. "And how would you feel if you found Will forcing a kiss on me in the woods?"

Mal would want to kill him, which was of course the answer Tom was counting on. He recited a Latin conjugation in his head before he trusted himself to speak. "I'd allow him the opportunity to apologize." Tom looked even more outraged. "*After* I'd beaten him bloody, of course." That seemed to mollify Tom a bit, and Mal had to smother a laugh. "And as I believe Arthur already carried out the first half of that, he's now moved on to the second. I'm as certain as I can be that he wants to reconcile."

Tom cast his eyes down again, and he worried at the edge of the blanket with a fingernail. "It's not just him. What about Owen? And — Caroline."

"You can see him," Mal said, very gently, answering Tom's real question, the one he couldn't bring himself to voice. Tom never mentioned his son. Though Mal had at length drawn it out of him that his child was a boy, it was all he'd known until Arthur had given him the child's name. "Arthur asked her."

A shudder went through Tom's body at that. "That's not possible," he said, but the naked hope in his voice was painful to hear.

"I promise you." Mal finally dared to wrap Tom in his arms and pull him close, pressing a kiss to the top of his head. "It'll take time. But she didn't say no."

Tom's exhale gusted against Mal's chest. "Will you want to — I don't know if you'd want to meet —"

"*Yes*," Mal said. "Wherever you go, I go. As long as you want me there."

"I do." Tom tipped his head back against Mal's shoulder. "Always."

"Do you forgive me, then? For writing back to Arthur? I think he couldn't bring himself to write to you directly. Too much pride."

Tom gave a shaky laugh. "That's Arthur. Honestly, I'd imagine Owen put him up to it. He's much better than Arthur deserves."

The little shock of jealousy that inspired surprised Mal enough that he couldn't hide it. Whatever Tom saw on his face made him sit up and kiss him, hard. "And you're better than I deserve," Tom added.

Mal eased him back down onto the pillows, stealing another kiss as he did. "I'll take that as forgiveness."

"Not at all," Tom said tartly, though the little smile playing over his lips belied it. "You'll need to earn that. At length."

"I look forward to it," Mal murmured against Tom's throat. He licked his way down, drawing out a moan. It ended in a little whimper as Mal reached Tom's chest and drew one of Tom's nipples between his lips, and Mal was achingly hard again. "Not much of a deterrent, if you don't want me to offend you again."

"I love you," Tom said. "I — don't stop." Because the

sound of those words never failed to take Mal's breath away, and he'd had to pause a moment, resting his cheek against Tom's soft skin, just savoring him.

Mal wrapped his hands around Tom's hips and looked up at him. "I love you. And I won't stop."

"I know damn well you won't." Tom's eyes narrowed, but his fond smile robbed his would-be sternness of any effect. "You wouldn't dare."

Mal laughed. "Oh, wouldn't I?" And he bent down to show Tom precisely how much he would dare, using his tongue to demonstrate. "Any further complaints?"

Tom moaned and wrapped his fingers in Mal's hair, pushing his head firmly down again. Mal chuckled into the tender skin of Tom's abdomen, earning him another moan and a curse. This might be the only way he'd ever win another argument, and he had no objections at all.

The End

The Reluctant Husband

Acknowledgements

My family is due some gratitude for their patience with my writing schedule. (The laundry is almost done, I promise. Not folded, maybe, but like, have you met me?)

Great thanks go to my thoughtful beta readers, Kassie and Brit. Without your critical eyes and kind encouragement, I might not have finished this one.

Very particular thanks to Kirk and Amy of LesCourt Author Services for your excellent critiques and eagle eyes. And thanks to the whole team!

Also, a shout-out to my wonderful online community, the Facebook group that shall not be named. Can there be a special exception for not talking about Fight Club if it's in the acknowledgements section of a book? You guys are the best.

Lastly but not at all leastly, Marika! As always, my most indefatigable, invaluable cheerleader. I shall repay you with a lifetime's supply of lemons and tea. May your praises be sung by all and sundry.

About the Author

Eliot is an editor by day and a romance writer by night, at least on a good day — more of a procrastinator by day and despairing eater of chocolate by night when inspiration doesn't flow and the day-job clients are being particularly insane. Go ahead and guess which of these is more common.

A steady childhood diet of pulp science fiction, classic tales of adventure, and romance novels surreptitiously borrowed from Eliot's grandmother eventually led to a writing career; Eliot picked up an M/M romance a few years ago and has been enjoying the genre as a reader and an author ever since.

Please get in touch — Eliot loves feedback from readers! Visit eliotgrayson.com, where you can find a newsletter sign-up and updates about upcoming releases, including excerpts. You can also follow Eliot on Goodreads.

If you enjoyed this book, please take a moment to leave a review on Amazon or Goodreads. Your opinions help other readers choose their next book. Thanks for reading!

Also in the Goddess-Blessed series

Available on Amazon for Kindle and in paperback

Goddess-blessed Owen Honeyfield is destined to enjoy perfect good fortune. The arrival of handsome and eligible Tom Drake in his country town appears to be the latest manifestation, and Tom's whirlwind proposal is the fulfillment of Owen's desires. When his betrothal takes a disastrous turn, Owen is left heartbroken and at the mercy of Arthur, Tom's disapproving elder brother. His reputation ruined and his bright future shattered, Owen must choose between loneliness and a marriage of convenience, with love no longer in reach.

Arthur Drake has always taken responsibility for Tom's scandalous behavior, but this time is worse — it isn't just the family name at stake, but his own happiness. When Tom's impulsive selfishness threatens to ruin the lives of everyone involved, Arthur has only one honorable choice. He'll need to repair the damage Tom has done and fight for his chance at love, knowing all the while he may never be able to take Tom's place in Owen's heart.

Reviews of *The Replacement Husband*

"I loved Arthur and his fierce need to protect Owen and his ability to remain steady in the midst of Owen's uncertainty. And that he laughed when Owen threw a pillow at his face."

– Kirstin at *Gay Book Reviews*

"…the book was fantastically written, it was romantic and sexy and sweet and I loved that the villain got his comeuppance. What more can you wish for?"

– Mari at *Bayou Book Junkie*

"This twist on the historical worked very well for me."

– Lucy at *Scattered Thoughts and Rogue Words*

Read on for an excerpt from
The Replacement Husband

THE MOORS SPREAD OUT on either side of him like an unrolled parchment. A particularly crumbly unrolled parchment, filled with the details of religious practices in ancient Pythia, perhaps. Although Pythia had at least been known for its fig wine and moonlit dances among the olive groves. Owen frowned. He was probably being rather too kind to Trewebury and its environs. If anyone could produce a single drop of fig wine within a hundred miles, he'd eat his unfashionably low-crowned hat.

And as for moonlit dances — Owen sniggered at the thought of his staid father, belly straining against his brown-striped waistcoat, cavorting in the moonlight. It would take a deal of fig wine to bring that about.

The moors had very little to recommend them, too, in any light. They had a certain bleak grandeur, Owen supposed, but mostly they had drizzle, and low, prickly bushes that caught at one's ankles, and the occasional surly sheep.

And Owen. He was there, seemingly for always, and seemingly always alone.

He could forget that, though, once he reached the cliffs that bounded the moors to the west. The glory of the ocean spread out before him seemed temptingly close despite the hundred feet of cliff-face that stood between him and it. Gulls swooped and wheeled, their calls echoing the shrill and terrifying cries of Mirreith, their patron goddess. And Owen's, due to the sigil she placed on his body while he was still in the womb. At least he had their company — the gulls and the goddess. Although the latter had been marked by her absence since troubling to claim him some decades before; Owen would have welcomed some sign of what her plan for him might be, even if that came in the form of a portentous seagull.

He watched for a little while, but the gulls did nothing but circle, occasionally diving down to examine some presumably delicious bit of slimy ocean detritus on the shore below. If the goddess meant him to take some meaning from that, he lacked the intelligence to discern it.

With a sigh, Owen turned back, away from the setting sun and toward home, where his parents would soon expect him for dinner. He tramped across the moors as often as he could escape on his own from his family's dull and respectable home, for there was simply nowhere else to go. Trewebury was more than a mere village; it was the local market town and busy enough in the mornings when tradesmen and farmers plied their services and wares in the central square and along the several streets that led into it. But it was entirely devoid of anything that could excite a young fellow of two-and-twenty with no interest in the girls who flocked to the market with their baskets.

Not that Owen would excite them, either. Trewebury was small enough that everyone knew of the goddess-touched in their midst. He wished, most passionately some days, that he could hide what he was. The town's young women either giggled at the very thought of him, or — often worse — thought to treat him as one of their own, an impulse he knew had its root in kindness, but one that left him feeling less of a man but not nearly a woman, either. He tried not to think of what the town's young men thought of him; if they thought of him at all, Owen suspected it was in terms he would not find flattering.

The sun sank deeper into the heavy bank of fog closing in from the sea, and the moor before him lost all its remaining color. One stray shaft of light still highlighted the top of a granite tor about a mile distant, the gently rolling swells of grass surrounding it only the gloomier and more featureless by contrast. It didn't matter. He knew this stretch of moor as well as he knew his own bedchamber.

Owen set a course just to the right of the tor, planning to scramble down a bit of hillside and meet the path that led around the foot rather than circling to it across flatter ground. Just as he reached the top of the slope, the sound of hoofbeats startled him out of his reverie, and he jumped, slipped, and with a cry, went tumbling down.

There was the scrape of gravel on his palms, and the slide of scree beneath his flailing legs; the ground and the sky whirled in a sickening dance, and then he landed flat on his back with a crunch, his head swimming. He blinked, and flinched as a few more bits of gravel pattered down.

When he blinked again, a dark, rather wavery shape blotted out what was left of the light. A giant frowning hat? That couldn't possibly be right. Owen tried to push himself up onto his elbows, only to be gently but firmly pushed back down again.

"Don't try to move," said a deep rasp of a voice. "You've most likely struck your head on something on the way down."

The shape removed its hat and resolved into a broad-shouldered gentleman, his face still too blurry to make out in detail — except for the outline of his expression. Of course. It was the man's face that was frowning. That made a great deal more sense.

Owen tried to laugh, felt very sick, and rolled to the side, retching and barely able to see, and then not seeing at all.

Also by Eliot Grayson

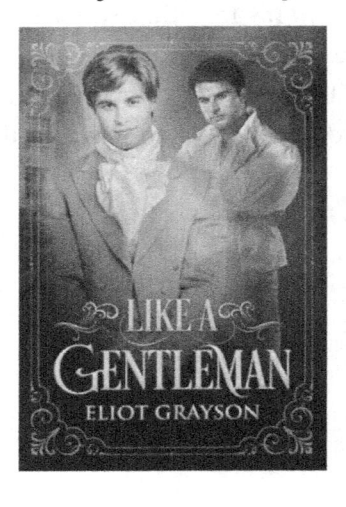

Available on Amazon for Kindle

When James Rowley, penniless nobleman and writer of sensational serials, discovers his story has been stolen, he takes himself to London to confront the man he believes to be responsible: Leo Wells, his editor. He means to have the truth, and he poses as a cruel fop to get it. But things aren't always what they seem.

Leo Wells has spent years pining for a man he knows only through letters and a portrait, and he's devastated to learn that the lovely James is nothing but a callous young aristocrat in a hideous pink waistcoat.

James takes his masquerade too far, behaving nothing at all like a gentleman. By the time he realizes his mistake, his plot for revenge may already have cost both men their one chance for happiness.

Reviews of *Like a Gentleman*

"…the events that follow are full of snark, humor, humiliation, passion, and repentance…Definitely recommended for fans of historical romance."
— *Lost in Love Book Blog*

"What an unexpected little gem this was. I do adore a good historical romance…"
— Jules at *The Novel Approach*

"…the chemistry between James and Leo was explosive. And there was some sweetness too. I couldn't ask for more."
— Stella at *Scattered Thoughts and Rogue Words*

Read on for an excerpt from *Like a Gentleman*

James flung the penny serial down on the scarred mahogany desk he'd rescued from the mold and mice of the north attic. Despite the chill that pervaded his little library and study, tucked away in the corner of the moldering ancestral mansion his sister-in-law condemned as positively Gothic, James flushed hot with fury. The bastard. The thieving, lying, hypocritical *bastard* had stolen his story, and here it was in black and white: *The Plucky Cartwright's Son*.

Did the knave think James didn't subscribe to his own publisher's competition? Both a thief and a bloody fool, it seemed.

James yanked out the bottom drawer of the desk, the jolt sending pens flying from the top and clattering onto the flagstone floor. He swore, yanked again, and pulled out heaps of correspondence until he found the letter he'd received when the manuscript was returned.

His editor's letters were typically short but biting, and this one, dated three months ago, was no exception. *Dear Mr. Rowley,* it read. *Regarding your last: our readers continue to prefer heroes whose ancestry includes at least a modicum of nobility. Such men may seem commonplace and dull to one accustomed to ornamenting the ton, but to those of us laboring down here in the muck of common trade — and most of our readership, along with your humble correspondent, can claim that dubious honor — an adventure carried out by a gentleman is more appealing. Might I suggest that your tale of the plucky cartwright's offspring's bold doings in Cairo could find a better home than Morton & Co., perhaps behind your fireplace grate? I shall hope to see your manuscript of* The Indian Duke *within the next month, as defined by the Gregorian calendar. As always, sir, I am your most obedient servant, L. Wells.*

What an ass. Even without the postscript, which set James to grinding his teeth to powder even though he'd already fumed over it months before: *P.S. I have included an example of said calendar for your reference. Note that next month comprises 31 days, with 24 hours each. A clock cost rather too much to post, so I can only pray you already possess one of those, though you have never given me any indication of such.*

The calendar in question had been burned in July; he could hardly crumple it and throw it in the fire again, much as he longed to do so.

James read the letter over again, feeding his rage until his heart pounded and his fists clenched, longing for a target. He exploded from his chair and frantically paced the length of the small room, picturing a bleeding and broken nose and wishing it belonged to the presumptuous, larcenous L. Wells. And what an idiotic way to sign his name, anyway. What *was* L. Wells's Christian name? Probably something dreadfully historical and pompous-sounding, like Leonidas. Serve the bastard right. James imagined L. Wells bent over a cluttered desk in a smoky office, grinning with malice as he copied out the manuscript, putting the copy in the post to another publisher at the same time he sent the original back to James with that blasted calendar. His graying hair would be standing out from his head in frizzy, messy locks, tobacco-stained fingers running through it as he shouted orders at his terrorized clerks.

James paused by the table in the corner to slosh a

generous portion of whisky into a glass and knock it back. The burn of it steadied him, and he poured another, drinking it more slowly. He had to consider his options calmly. The Earl of Winthrop, also known as James's brother Rodney, could crush L. Wells like an insect if he chose; the great irony was that a Rowley sinking to penning sensational stories for money would give the earl hysterics, and so that avenue for redress was utterly closed.

Perhaps that should be his next tale: *The Hysterical Earl*. L. Wells might like that. He might not like it as much when James stuffed the manuscript down his mocking, plebeian throat...a pleasant fantasy, but that would require going to London, where the potential wealthy wives Rodney loved to throw at him lurked in every drawing room, ready to sink their fangs in a man and drag him down to an underworld of announcements in the *Post* and morning visits and silk bonnets...James shuddered. L. Wells at least likely didn't wear bonnets — although James would no longer put it past the fellow.

Thoughts of London sparked an idea in the back of James's mind, and he swallowed another mouthful of liquor, mulling it over. He would have to visit Morton & Co. in person if he wanted to get his due, but whether that would involve credit for the story he'd written, the money L. Wells had made from it, or simply the man's face at the end of James's fist could be determined later.

But did his editor know who he was? James had been fool enough to use his real name in his correspondence, naïve as he had been when he first entertained the idea of writing to supplement his dwindling allowance, though he had retained enough presence of mind to provide a *nom de plume* for publication. If L. Wells had thought to look him up in Debrett's, and the jab about ornamenting the ton implied he at least suspected James's station, he might believe James would ignore the theft to avoid a scandal. In that case this smacked unpleasantly of blackmail, even if indirectly. Or perhaps the editor simply thought James would never find out.

Either way, James had only one card to play: his rank. He would beard the lion in his foul den and overwhelm him with a display of arrogance. These sorts of revolutionary aristocrat-hating *hoi polloi* were always the ones most susceptible to a fellow coming the great lord, and James, usually just as happy to drink ale with the local yeoman farmers in their well-scrubbed kitchens as to go visiting with his brother, longed to put L. Wells in his place. Make the fellow grovel a bit. And hope to God L. Wells didn't call his bluff, because damn him, he was quite right if he thought James couldn't afford to make his brother the laughingstock of the House of Lords.

In the meantime, he'd need to manufacture a reason for his visit to the publisher's office, where he'd never before set foot. James ran his hands over his newest manuscript, of which half was already cleanly copied and ready. That would do.

Leo waited until the last sounds of departing typesetters and clerks faded away into the foggy November night before throwing himself back in his creaking chair and groaning his frustration aloud. He'd been suppressing a fit ever since the morning post had brought nothing. Again. At least, nothing from James

Rowley, which, in Leo's state of near-obsession, amounted to nothing at all. Rowley's latest effort had arrived a fortnight since in a bundle of brown paper and string, two days early, but with at least half of it missing. Leo's reply had been a masterwork of reverse snobbery and insult. He had been certain he would receive an immediate tirade by return post.

Each time he wrote to Rowley, he waited on tenterhooks for the earliest possible moment that could bring a reply; he'd grown adept at schooling his face into indifference when he received one so as not to cause gossip among the clerks. Now, he wished he had that trouble, rather than this gnawing anxiety over the lack of a letter.

The first three years of correspondence had been easier. He'd known that James Rowley was too foolish to use a false name when writing to a publisher of sensational serials, and that he had a gift for writing an entertaining tale that sold. His stories made Leo chuckle, and always charmed him, but they exchanged only manuscript packages and brief, businesslike notes. It was just after the third year of working together when Leo had been glancing through the latest Debrett's and "Rowley" had caught his eye. Of course it couldn't be...but there, listed as the fourth Earl of Winthrop's second son, was a James Rowley. Leo's author had his mail held at the coaching inn of a Gloucestershire village. It took only a moment longer with a map to determine that the village sat just half a mile outside the family estate's walls.

Not long after that Leo recalled he'd long promised an old friend a visit — an old friend who happened to live in Canterbury. A coincidence, of course, that Canterbury was a mere nine miles from Winthrop Court. And that Leo's stay happened to include a Wednesday, on which the house opened for tours given by a housekeeper who looked a little askance at Leo's overlong and unfashionably unstyled black hair but allowed him in anyway, perhaps thinking that a man in a sedately tailored olive coat couldn't be entirely disreputable.

Leo bit back his seething impatience as Mrs. Green took the small group of visitors through endless ballrooms, parlors, libraries, and conservatories. At long last, she led them up yet another set of marble stairs and into the portrait gallery, a long room with a row of windows down one side and what seemed a hundred massive paintings in gilt frames lining the opposite wall. He sidestepped Mrs. Green, who seemed determined to spend the rest of the bloody year droning on about the oak parquetry floor, and went at once to the other end of the hall where the most recent family portraits hung.

Nothing could have prepared him for what he saw. The late fourth earl had been a tall, commanding man, and the elder son was his image, blocky and dark with blue eyes and an arrogant set to his chin. But that wasn't what made Leo's breath catch in his chest.

On the other side of the fourth earl, caught perfectly in a mischievous half-smile by the genius who had painted the portrait, stood a slender, golden-haired Adonis, whose deep dark eyes gloriously contrasted with his fair coloring. He'd inherited his father's height, but the rest must have come from the stunning blonde, certainly the fourth countess, whose portrait hung beside the family group.

And that was that. Leo was lost before he even drew

his next ragged breath.

Furious with the unkindness of fate, with the beautiful James Rowley and his damned little smile that seemed to promise everything Leo had ever desired and could never possess, and most of all with himself, he'd written an uncharacteristically sharp reply to Rowley's most recent note. The return post brought him a longer letter than he'd ever had from the man. And if every word of that letter dripped with disdain, at least it meant Rowley spared him a thought. Pathetic, he knew. Still, he wrote back in kind, savoring each page he received as a sign of Rowley's attention and knowing all the while that each exchange left him lower and lower in Rowley's esteem.

The next two years were pure torture.

Every terse, hostile letter from James — Rowley, he must think of him as Rowley — had been written by the white hand that rested so casually on James's — *dammit* — slim hip in that blasted painting. The thought of that hand holding a pen, holding anything, left Leo aching, hiding behind his desk until his arousal subsided. Perhaps James had set the pen in its holder, absently toying with it, long delicate fingers sliding up and down its hard length…Leo flopped back in his chair, grateful for his solitude, and pinched the bridge of his nose.

This had gone far enough. Bad enough to be distracted by, all right, obsessed with, a man he'd never met and likely never would. James was the son of an earl, and Leo, whose father owned a tavern in Portsmouth, really had no business even reading Debrett's, let alone longing for a nobleman whose name inscribed one of its pages. James was so far above his touch he might as well have come from a distant star.

The thought of James and touching at once would lead to Leo unbuttoning his trousers and taking his throbbing length in hand, and that way lay madness. He took up his hat and coat and left the office, slamming every door so hard the frame shook. No more work would be done that evening. Damn James Rowley anyway.

Made in the USA
Monee, IL
31 January 2025